A
Harlequin
Romance

LAKE OF SILVER

by

BELINDA DELL

HARLEQUIN BOOKS   TORONTO
WINNIPEG

Original hard cover edition published in 1974
by Mills & Boon Limited.

© Belinda Dell 1974

SBN 373-01846-0

Harlequin edition published January 1974

Printed in Canada

CHAPTER I

The lift doors glided open. Clarissa stepped out into the grey-carpeted corridor. She had only once been on this floor of the Pagel Building—the day she arrived and was interviewed by the Personnel Officer. Once again she was headed for that selfsame office, but this time to receive her parting instructions.

She paused outside the door to smooth a hand over her hair. It wasn't that she was nervous, not a bit. It was simply that her browny-gold thatch was so unmanageably soft that even the breeze of her own movement could make it flutter out of place. She glanced at her watch: ten-forty-five precisely. She turned the handle and went in.

'Miss Oakley?' said the assistant. 'Please go straight in. Mrs James is expecting you.'

Mrs James had a folder of papers on her desk, together with various envelopes and packets.

'Good morning, Miss Oakley. Do sit down. It's a lovely day for your trip.'

'Yes indeed,' Clarissa murmured, forbearing to point out that as she wasn't flying to Switzerland until nearly midnight, the weather at mid-morning was of very little account.

'I have all your documentation ready,' said Mrs James, picking up the envelope immediately beneath her right hand. 'Here is your plane ticket, and here is a supply of currency to meet your travelling expenses. You can either take the airport bus from Geneva Airport to Cornavin Station, or you can take a taxi all the way to the Rue des Collegiers, which is only a little distance further on, on the other side of the river.'

'River?' said Clarissa. 'That will be the Rhône?'

'Quite correct. The Rue des Collegiers isn't far from St Peter's. I think you'll like it—when I stayed there some years ago I found it quite charming.'

Clarissa nodded. She knew that quite a few of the London staff had done a tour of duty with the parent

5

firm, Entreprise Pagel, of Switzerland; the company took a quite paternal interest in the welfare of its employees, supplying them with accommodation if need be. Since Clarissa had no previous contacts, she was to share an apartment in Geneva with a Swiss girl.

Mrs James took up one of the small packages. 'Here is the key to the apartment. Aimée Regenbach is on holiday until the twenty-eighth, so you'll have to manage on your own for a few days. Think you'll be all right?'

'Oh, I think so. So long as there's a kettle and some instant coffee, I'll be quite happy. I can buy bread and so forth in the morning.'

'That won't be necessary,' Mrs James said on a faint note of reproof. 'The *concierge* will see to it that there's something in the larder for you to eat, and if you want anything you only have to knock on her door—she has the apartment on the ground floor at the back.'

'I see. Thank you.'

'Here is a travel pass for the Geneva bus service. You may prefer to walk to work—it's only a few minutes away.'

'Quai Général Guison,' Clarissa murmured.

'Precisely. And that brings me to an important point, Miss Oakley. Having worked in the London branch for a year you're well aware that the Geneva office starts work at eight o'clock sharp. You will be punctual, won't you?'

'Of course.'

'I only mention it,' said Mrs James with a tinge of anxiety, 'because it seems your predecessor came to grief on that particular point. She couldn't quite . . . er . . . acclimatise to such an early start.'

Privately, Clarissa thought that her predecessor hadn't been given long in which to make the change-over. Little more than a month ago, the vacancy had been posted on the staff notice-board: 'French-speaking English secretary, good speeds, willing to travel. Required to handle Monsieur Pagel's London-bound correspondence immediately.' Details of salary and benefits had followed, together with instructions to apply at once.

Clarissa knew, as did everyone else in the London

office, that the identical notice had appeared earlier in the year—which could only mean that the girl who applied then had either given notice or been dismissed. Groups of typists and secretaries had sat in the staff cafeteria, discussing the situation. 'The man's a positive ogre,' said the girls who'd been with the Pagel Company long enough to tune in on the bush-telegraph.

Undeterred, a lively and enthusiastic Devonian had applied—and a few weeks later, there was the job again, at the head of the noticeboard.

'What does he *do* to secretaries?' the typing pool asked each other. 'Eat them?'

Everyone thought Clarissa had gone out of her mind when she sent in her application. If big, perky Jenny Trevelyan couldn't hold down the job, what chance had a little sparrow like Clarissa?

Nevertheless she held out against all attempts to dissuade her. It was all part of The Plan—the plan to improve herself. She'd been just over twelve months in the Pagel Building, and she was tired of being a general dogsbody to three young executives. Even if Monsieur Roland Pagel was a tyrant, he was only *one* tyrant—she was fed up with trying to satisfy three masters. Besides, the money was much better and it offered a chance to live abroad. Why else had she spent evenings at language school keeping her French at a good colloquial level? Why else had she read the magazines and journals of the construction industry from cover to cover? Why else had she invested money in having her floppy hair expensively styled, her make-up specially chosen?'

For her career, that was why. She was going to be a success. It was important.

She came from a family of cheerful failures. Her mother made wine which was left in corners to mature and got forgotten. Her father taught music to a succession of bored, tone-deaf pupils. Her elder brother served in a supermarket and spent his weekends listening to pop groups. She alone—the cuckoo in the nest, a source of bewilderment to all the others—wanted to organise her life, to achieve something. With very little help from anyone else she had made her way from her home town in Northumberland to London, where she'd progressed from a filing job in an engineering firm to a typing job in a surveyor's office until, triumphantly, she had entered the prestigious Pagel Building as a junior secretary.

Now she was moving out into a different world. The Pagel Company of London was big business, certainly, but it was staffed by people like herself, who spoke the same language, watched the same television programmes, ate the same breakfast foods, and shared the same cultural background.

In Geneva it would be different. She would have to stand on her own two feet. But it was part of the plan. The plan required that by the time she was twenty-five she would be living and working abroad; she had made it with a year to spare. The next step was to spend two years, perhaps three, in gaining experience. By the age of twenty-eight she wanted to move to another country where, she hoped, she would have charge of a department. Entreprise Pagel, the Swiss parent firm, already had an office in Brussels and another in Milan. Her sights were set on one of those.

No matter how crotchety and bad-tempered old Monsieur Pagel turned out to be, she'd put up with him. After all, she was only being hired to handle the English letters; she would stay out of his way as much as possible. She wouldn't be late in the mornings, she wouldn't be a clock-watcher in the evenings.

'You do understand,' Mrs James was saying, 'that you may have to move about if Monsieur Pagel requires you. He has a house at the other end of the Lake Geneva from which he sometimes works, and there's an office in Zurich too.'

'I'm quite prepared for that, Mrs James.'

'That's excellent . . .' The Personnel Officer fiddled with her glasses. 'Is there anything you'd like to ask me . . . er . . . about the job?'

Clarissa wondered what she would say if she asked: 'Is Monsieur Pagel really an ogre?' Suppressing a smile, she said instead, 'I think I'll just take it as it comes, Mrs James, thank you.'

'Perhaps that's best. And in any case Aimée Regenbach can fill you in on any details. She's a computer programmer in the Planning Department, a very nice girl from all I can gather.'

They shook hands. Clarissa had a feeling that Mrs James was trying to convey something to her, but whether commiseration or reassurance, she couldn't quite tell.

As she came out into the corridor the door of the Salaries Office opened and the very girl whom Clarissa was replacing, Jenny Trevelyan, came towards her.

'Hello, I didn't know you were back,' Clarissa said.

'Only momentarily, to collect my insurance cards and so forth.' The other girl gave her a puzzled stare. 'Is it true what I hear—that you're filling the vacancy?'

'Quite true. I'm just going home to finish my packing, then I fly to Geneva tonight.'

Jenny shook her head. 'I give you ten days. Twelve at the most. He'll bite your head off on the first day, and chew up the rest by the end of the month.'

'Thanks a million! You're a great help.'

'Don't go, Clarissa. It's *such* hard work, and he expects superhuman efforts without any let-up. And he never says "thank you" or "would you mind"!'

Clarissa's face lit up with her sudden, spontaneous smile. 'Maybe he feels he doesn't have to since he's already paying you to do the job. I've met bosses like that before.'

'Not like this one, you haven't! He's just impossible—'

'I refuse to be put off, Jenny. I've got my air ticket and the key to the apartment—'

'And in two weeks' time you'll have a perpetual headache and a great desire to come home! You can try any tactics you like—you'll find Pagel impossible to handle.'

'There must be some way to build up a relationship—'

'Not that I know of. The girl before me had done everything he ordered, making herself a proper doormat —and he walked over her. So when I took over I tried treating him firmly. The result is I only lasted half as long as Marjorie. I can't imagine *you'll* succeed where everybody else has failed.'

'Perhaps not,' Clarissa admitted, her uncertainty returning in the face of the other girl's bitterness. 'All the same . . . I'm going to Geneva.'

The problems began even before she got there. Her flight was delayed by an electrical fault, so that it was one o'clock in the morning when they landed. She took a taxi straight to the Rue des Collegiers; from its windows she could see the tips of the high mountains gleaming under a moonlit sky. Their route took them down the Rue du Mont Blanc, almost deserted at that hour but sparkling nevertheless from the lights in the boutique windows.

Then, so unexpected that it took her breath away, they were crossing a bridge and the lake was gleaming on her left hand. It stretched away, unbelievably lovely, a sheet of shimmering silver on which swans drifted like small white galleons in full sail. The scent of flowers drifted to her—roses, verbena, other perfumes that seemed more exotic. The night air was cool; a faint breeze stirred the trees on the quays that bordered the water, causing the boats to curtsey on the waves.

'It's beautiful,' she murmured to the taxi-driver.

'*Mademoiselle dit?*'

'*C'est beau,*' she said. '*Très beau . . .*'

He nodded. '*Ah, oui, c'est pas mauvais, notre p'tit lac,*' he agreed. 'We quite like our little lake, *mademoiselle.*'

He carried her suitcase up to the door of the third floor apartment. 'Quite a climb,' he said, puffing. '*Mais nous sommes montagnards, quoi!*'

She would have liked to tell him that though the Swiss were mountaineers, she was not. But by now the excitement that had kept her awake was wearing off, so that a vast weariness seemed to be waiting to engulf her. She paid him and thanked him and went inside. The apartment, glimpsed through a veil of fatigue, seemed pleasant enough. She went across the living-room to look in at one door: that room had personal belongings arranged in it. She tried the next door: a bed gleaming in the moonlight, the coverlet neatly turned back.

She found her overnight bag, removed her make-up, managed ten strokes of the brush on her soft, unmanageable hair, and fell into bed.

The sounds that woke her were loudly metallic—clankings and bangings. A motor engine started up.

None of this would have mattered if it hadn't been that it seemed to come from right under her pillow, and when she prised an eye open to look at her watch she discovered the time was five a.m.

Still drugged with sleep, yet with an erupting indignation, she clambered out of bed. The room was full of a clear, sharp light. She staggered to the window. The sun was up, but not far enough to overtop the slopes of the mountains, so that the sky was a vault of pearly gold reflecting into brilliance on the city below.

Immediately below her window there was a huge building site. Tall boarding protected the area from the passers-by and the passers-by from any dangers. Within the wooden boundary, deep foundations had been dug—Clarissa knew that this meant a very tall building would be erected on the site.

Deep in this sunken arena, a bright blue dump-truck was busily moving from point to point on the floor of crushed rock. All that she could see of the driver, from directly above, was the top of his white protective helmet and the shoulders of a dark blue shirt. He was hard at work.

At five in the morning!

'Hi, you!' shouted Clarissa.

The little truck buzzed fussily away to the far side of the site.

'Hi!' She opened the window wider, to lean out a little. But it was useless. From so far up, and masked by the noise of his motor, her voice couldn't reach him.

She closed the window, went back to bed, lay down. The sounds from below were completely audible. She rolled over, pulling her pillow over her ears. The dump-truck revved its engine, then came roaring over to the near side of the area.

'Oh, this is outrageous!' She sat up. She'd only had four hours' sleep. Tired with annoyance, she leapt up, dragged her dressing-gown from her case, and as she pulled it on made for the door. Mindful of the other occupants of the building, who might still be sleeping, she went quietly, her slippered feet silent on the stone stairs.

The outside door had been left unlatched for her last night. Now it appeared to be locked, and for a moment she couldn't fathom how to unlock it until she discovered a lever on the wall of the vestibule. When she came out into the lane the cool morning breeze off the lake caught at the flounced edge of her cambric dressing-gown; she drew it close about her and tied the sash tight as she hurried to the open gate of the construction area.

From the big gateway a slope had been left so that machinery could be taken in and out. Once in, everything presumably had to be lowered by the huge tower crane looming on the far side, for the slope came to an abrupt end at the edge of the big square pit; only a few ladders had been fixed for humans to scamper up and down.

Clarissa certainly didn't fancy going down a ladder to the muddy terrain below. In fact, now that her first flush of indignation was subsiding, she felt rather foolish, out at dawn in the alleys of a foreign city and clad only in a nightdress and dressing-gown. True, the dressing-gown was of fine white cotton sprigged with violets and edged with crochet lace—in effect rather like the long Victorian dresses fashionable for evening wear. All the same, she began to feel absurd.

But just as she was turning to retreat back to the doorway of the apartment building, a head in a white safety helmet suddenly came over the edge of the excavation, to be followed by shoulders clad in dark blue sailcloth. The driver of the dump-truck was climbing up to street level.

He gave an exclamation of surprise at seeing her. Then he said something in an abrupt, questioning tone. The language was unknown to Clarissa—she guessed it to be the Swiss-French dialect. As she hesitated, wondering whether to turn and hurry away or to reply, and if the latter whether to speak in English or French, the man seemed to realise that she hadn't understood.

'What are you doing here?' he demanded in perfect

French. 'This is private property. You can read, surely?' He nodded at the big placard on the open gate, which stated 'No Entry'.

'I can not only read, I can hear, too. I came to—'

'If you're on your way home from a party,' he interrupted, eyeing the sprigged dressing-gown, 'you've taken a wrong turning, young lady.'

'A party?' Clarissa echoed, bewildered. 'I was in bed sound asleep! I didn't get to bed till nearly two, and you woke—'

'If you enjoy staying out until the early hours of the morning and fall into bed without taking off your party dress, that's your affair. But don't extend your eccentricity into wandering round excavations—'

'Eccentricity! *You're* the one that's eccentric, starting work at this unearthly hour! I suppose you're being paid double rates, or maybe even treble—'

'As a matter of fact, no. I came to look at the safety precautions. And speaking of safety, you might have had a serious accident, walking into the working area in that ridiculous apparel. Haven't you any sense?'

Clarissa was speechless with indignation. She stared at her antagonist. Who did he think he was, berating her like this? By all the rules of normal behaviour he should be apologizing for having disturbed her sleep at this hour of the morning. But there wasn't the least sign of contrition on his lean, angular face, and his severe brows were drawn together in disapproval.

He had swung himself over the top of the ladder and was now standing on the entry slope, looking down from his considerable height at her small, dishevelled figure. She was suddenly aware that her hair was all awry and that she had no make-up on. She blushed and turned away.

'I shall complain to your foreman,' she muttered. 'It's extremely inconsiderate to run noisy machinery so early.' A thought struck her. 'It's Saturday, too!'

'What has that to do with it?' The cool greeny-grey eyes lit up with a sudden understanding. 'Oh, of course. *Le weekend!* That's what your accent has been telling me —you're English. Well, let me inform you, Mademoiselle

Anglaise, work will begin on this site today as usual, at seven o'clock. This is an important building project—'

'Oh, you're impossible!' Clarissa said, walking away.

The slope up to the gateway wasn't very pleasant to walk on in thin slippers, for its surface was made of crushed rock. As she was a yard or so from the entry, a particularly sharp edge seemed about to cut through the soles; she changed her footing too hastily, became entangled in her long skirt, and would have fallen—if a man hadn't providentially appeared in the opening and caught her.

'Well!' he said in surprised amusement. 'I didn't expect to have a model supplied—!'

Clarissa regained her balance just in time to prevent herself colliding with the heavy camera-carrier slung from his shoulder.

'I'm sorry,' she gasped, 'the stones are so uneven.'

'Are you all right?'

'Yes, thank you.' She drew away from his arms, which he rather unwillingly opened to allow her to go free.

From behind her the other man spoke. 'Good heavens, this place is getting to be like Cornavin Station—!'

'Good morning,' said the man with the camera. 'I'm Jean-Louis Blech. I have permission to take photographs—' He took a letter from the breast pocket of his windcheater. 'You're the site foreman?'

'Ah yes,' said the other, glancing at the letter and handing it back, 'it was on your behalf I was checking the area. But you're earlier than I expected.'

'Well, the light is so good at the moment—'

'If you'll excuse me,' Clarissa said, moving past him. 'Thank you for appearing at the right moment—'

'Just a minute,' he said, catching at her sleeve. 'What are you doing here, *mademoiselle?*'

'I came out to complain.' She nodded towards the doorway of the apartment building. 'But I've wasted my time, it seems.'

'Please let me escort you. The cobblestones are uneven.' He offered his arm in an extravagant gesture of gallantry and she, with an amused smile, accepted it.

14

'My name is Jean-Louis, as you heard,' he said. 'Please tell me yours.'

'Clarissa. Clarissa Oakley.'

'And please tell me what you intend to do to console yourself now that your complaint has gone unheard?'

She shrugged. 'I don't know. It's useless to try to go back to sleep, I imagine. I suppose I'd better start the day . . .'

'That's an excellent idea. Let me help you start it. I have to take some shots of the equipment over there—' he jerked his head towards the excavation. 'But in about an hour I shall have finished. May I call and take you to breakfast?'

'Take me to breakfast! At six o'clock in the morning? Where, for goodness' sake?'

'Ah, you forget, this is Switzerland, *mademoiselle*. I know a very cosy little café where the *croissants* melt in the mouth, and the black cherry jam is home-made. May I take you there?'

'Oh . . . well . . . I don't really know . . .' But his words had made her realise that she was ravenously hungry. She had no idea what she might find in the larder of her apartment, but there would certainly be no freshly-baked *croissants*. 'Very well,' she agreed. 'I should love to have breakfast at your café.'

'Splendid. In about an hour, then, Clarissa.'

They were at the outside door of the building. She turned to smile a goodbye before going inside. Over Jean-Louis' shoulder she caught a glimpse of the site foreman standing in the fence-gateway and gazing at them. There was no mistaking the sardonic disapproval on his face.

Once upstairs in the apartment, Clarissa turned on the bathwater and while the tub filled, did her unpacking. Sunshine was now coming in strongly at the big casement window, so she decided to wear a sleeveless dress of butter yellow, with which she matched a bracelet and earrings of amber. She took time over her make-up, decided to protect her unruly hair with a silk kerchief patterned with leopard spots, and on the whole wasn't dissatisfied with the results when at last she went downstairs to meet

15

Jean-Louis.

The *concierge* was already up and about, sweeping vigorously with a square-headed broom. '*B'jour, mademoiselle!*' she chirped, bustling forward to introduce herself as Madame Lallais. She was clearly a very conscientious caretaker, eager to serve Clarissa in every possible way, but Clarissa gently refused her offers to do her shopping for her and attend to such things as hiring a bicycle or a car.

'Thank you, *madame*, but I'd like to learn how to look after myself,' she explained. 'It's part of the fun of being abroad.'

Madame Lallais was about to argue, but broke off in astonishment as Jean-Louis appeared in the doorway.

'*Ma foi*, she has not wasted any time, that one!' Clarissa heard her say to herself as they went out.

At Jean-Louis's side Clarissa walked eagerly down the narrow cobbled lane. Over the housetops she could see the spire of the cathedral glinting in the sun's rays.

'Did you say you were taking photographs on the building site?' she queried.

'Yes, I'm a commercial photographer. The pictures have been commissioned by the makers of the machinery —for an advertising brochure, I think. Very dull, really, although there's a strength and solidarity about them that is rather agreeable.'

'Did you get what you wanted?'

'More or less. The disagreeable character in the helmet was quite knowledgeable about which machine did what, but on the whole he got in the way, so I sent him to have breakfast and he didn't reappear. I got on a lot faster after that, I'm happy to say. I shouldn't have liked to be late for our date.'

'Where are we going, by the way?'

'Just the other side of the Rhône. There's a little turning off the Place St Gervais. So now . . .' He paused to take her hand and, holding her at arm's length, survey her. 'What are you doing in Geneva, Clarissa Oakley?'

'I've come to work in an office. It's quite ordinary, really—I've been transferred from the London branch.'

She explained how she came to take the job. He listened attentively, his head a little on one side. He had a narrow, clever face, with bright black eyes that missed very little. As she reached the end of her short explanation he tucked her arm in his and said: 'Well, for my part I'm very glad the other girl gave up the job, because it brought you here. This morning when I saw you in your strangely romantic clothes against that background of mechanical contraptions, do you know—I felt the strangest sensation! As if you had come to me out of a dream . . .'

They reached the bank of the river. Traffic was moving fast here; trams and buses were busy, with groups of passengers alighting in this active business quarter already although it was still, by Clarissa's standards, very early. Small shops were beginning to open; shutters were being taken down, roller shutters were being pushed up, the florist was setting out flowering plants and watering them from a bright red watering-can. On the river, boatmen were readying their craft for the day's hirings. To the east, the Lake of Geneva stretched away, a sparkling expanse of steely-blue under the early morning sky.

As they walked across the Coulouvrenière Bridge, the warmth of the July morning was tempered by the little wind from the lake. It tugged at the scarf covering Clarissa's hair, so that she had to hold on to it.

'There's almost always a breeze off the lake,' Jean-Louis commented. He zipped up his black windcheater with a shrug of annoyance. 'I hate it. One day when I've collected enough capital I'm going to move to the South Seas and set up business there.'

Clarissa laughed. 'I bet the wind blows in the South Seas sometimes.'

'But not a cold wind. And in the winter there's no snow.' He cast a glance of dislike towards the peaks of the Alps on the south shore of the lake. Clarissa realised with some surprise that he was serious about moving to the tropics—he genuinely had no liking for this lovely valley and its gentle city on the lake shore.

Then it occurred to her that she, too, had wanted to

get away. A restlessness like his had made her leave her family and her home in the north for London where, quite soon, she had lifted her eyes to see farther horizons. She felt a kinship with Jean-Louis; she too had felt the impulse to move on, to find a better place where her life could expand and come to flower. True, she had no particular urge to rush off to the South Seas; she had the feeling that secretaries weren't much in demand there. But each man has his own El Dorado, his land of gold, and for Jean-Louis it was a palm-girt island where the *föhn* wind never blew, where the mountains were always clothed in lush green and never knew the sparkle of winter snow.

She gave him a friendly smile. 'I hope you get there,' she said. 'Speaking for myself, I'm more than satisfied with what I see around me.'

'Oh . . . Switzerland . . .' He hunched his shoulders. 'It's so claustrophobic! Always mountains frowning down at you, and the entire country is hemmed in on every side by powerful neighbours—France, Germany, Italy. It's impossible to feel free in Switzerland—it's impossible to find elbow-room.'

Clarissa felt she had no right to argue with him, but she had only to glance towards the mountain slopes in the distance to see that there was room a-plenty—vast expanses of empty rock and crag where a man could feel free. She sensed that the freedom he meant was psychological.

'I've always thought of this country as being rather special—'

'Special? It certainly is! The entire population is only devoted to the making of money! They think of nothing else—it's what we're famous for, the Swiss banks.'

'Now, now,' she admonished gently. 'You're talking like that famous bit from the film where someone said Switzerland's only contribution to the world was the cuckoo clock. It's absolutely untrue. Switzerland gave us the Red Cross, and the example of people of different languages and culture—French, German and Italian—living together in harmony.'

'You'll learn,' he said. 'It only succeeds because we

tie ourselves up with ridiculous rules and conventions. Look at us now!' They had reached the far side of the bridge and were waiting on the lakeside to cross to the other pavement of the Quai Turettini. 'Not a single car in sight, but we all stand here like a bunch of sheep waiting for the traffic signal to change so that we can cross! And why? Because the regulation says it's an offence to cross the road unless the green pedestrian light comes on!'

He took her arm and was about to thrust her forward on to the crossing, but the traffic signals foiled him by changing so that the group of a dozen people trotted across with them.

'You see?' he said in mock despair. 'Like a bunch of sheep!'

Clarissa laughed. 'You may be right in all you say,' she admitted, 'but I'm too hungry to care!'

The café to which he took her was quite big and obviously popular. Young people with duffle bags or rucksacks were congregated in corners, poring over maps. Clarissa recalled that this was a university city with a large quota of student-visitors, and certainly the babble of conversation was in a variety of tongues. Jean-Louis led her past the busy area by the window, to a corner where the habitués—business people on their way to work—were sitting quietly eating breakfast while they read the morning paper. The waiter, without being asked, arrived with a tray laden with a plate of *croissants*, a little pot of jam, another of butter, and large cups. When he had set these before them, he hustled away to return a moment later with jugs of black coffee and hot milk.

He said to Jean-Louis: 'Had an assignment this morning?'

'On the site at the Rue des Collegiers—construction machinery.'

'Ah yes—the new hotel. My brother's hoping to take charge of the kitchens there once it's built. How's it going?'

'Only the foundations so far, Henri.'

'Oh, well, it'll soon start to grow. You know what

Pagel is like.'

'Pagel? Is he the contractor?'

The waiter nodded. 'Didn't you see it in *Vingt-quatre Heures*? There was a feature about it. He's guaranteed to have it finished in a year and a half. The Chaval Hotel chain are due to open it in June of next year, and if Pagel has promised it'll be ready, it'll be ready.'

When he had gone to serve another customer, Clarissa said, 'I'd no idea the site was under the control of Entreprise Pagel!'

'Why should you?' Jean-Louis said, buttering a *croissant*.

'It so happens that's the firm I've come to work for.'

'No! Really? This dreadful tyrant you've come to work for—it's Roland Pagel?'

She nodded.

'I don't envy you. I've never met him, but they say he's a man of iron. All he thinks about is putting up huge buildings and making money—in fact he's a perfect example of what I was complaining about a moment ago. No soul, no emotions—only a profit-and-loss account for a heart.'

'How can you be so sure, if you've never met him?' she countered. She had an obscure urge to defend her employer. 'As a matter of fact, although he's an awful old curmudgeon, he does look after his employees awfully well.'

'Only because it's good business to do so, I bet. If they fall ill or have welfare problems they're less efficient and then business would suffer.'

By this time she was busily engaged in pouring the coffee. 'Have it your own way,' she said, too enchanted by the appetising smell to care about the reputation of old Roland Pagel.

They made a leisurely breakfast. Jean-Louis hadn't been exaggerating when he said the *croissants* melted in the mouth, a fact which encouraged Clarissa to eat three. The newspapers hanging on rods near the coat-rack intrigued her. Jean-Louis brought two, so that they could read at their ease over their third cup of coffee. No one hurried them; customers came and went, the sunshine outside strengthened, the proprietor opened the front door and set tables out on the pavement. It was still not quite eight o'clock, yet on the opposite side of the street the shops were open for business. To Clarissa it was so entirely different from the London rush hour that she felt exhilarated and liberated. How could Jean-Louis possibly feel hemmed in?

'What would you like to do now?' he inquired as they came out of the café.

'Haven't you got business to attend to?' she replied. 'I don't want to take up your time—'

'Nonsense, nonsense.' He tapped the camera bag as he slung it on his shoulder. 'I have to develop this film and do the proofs for Monday, but that's no problem. What would be a good idea is to drop this bag into my car—that's in the underground car park. Then I can show you around Geneva. Would you like that?'

'That would be lovely.'

The car park proved to be not only underground but underwater—it had been built in a huge excavation hollowed out beneath the Lake of Geneva. There was a good deal of coming and going as Saturday shoppers arrived to visit the big stores in the Place du Molard while travellers edged their way out to begin their journey home. When they came up again to street level Clarissa noticed a luxurious open roadster nosing its way out of the exit from the car park into the traffic on the Quai. What attracted her attention was the driver—or rather her clothes, for Clarissa was very fashion-conscious.

The girl in the Lamborghini was wearing a superbly-cut shirt in a very soft silk, its colour the most brilliant and striking pink Clarissa had ever seen. She was just saying to herself that the shirt must have cost a fortune —for to tailor severely a silk so fine is expert work— when the roadster turned into the main thoroughfare. In doing so, the passenger in the right-hand seat became visible.

Clarissa gave a gasp of astonishment.

'What's the matter?' asked Jean-Louis.

Too surprised to speak, Clarissa pointed. The passenger in this obviously expensive car driven by this

21

obviously expensive girl was none other than the work-man who had been driving the dump-truck on the building site at five in the morning.

Attracted by her pointing gesture, he turned his head. No longer covered by the safety helmet, his hair was revealed as medium brown streaked with grey. He looked more distinguished, more authoritative, even though there was rock-dust on the collar of the blue shirt.

She received a long, cold stare from the grey-green eyes. Then the traffic moved, the Lamborghini surged forward, and he was gone.

'Well!' said Jean-Louis. 'He's got expensive taste in women, our *ouvrier!*'

'I simply c-couldn't believe my eyes!' she stammered.

He grinned. 'Perhaps we should say that the lady has inexpensive taste in men,' he suggested. 'In cars and clothes, only the best is good enough. Did you see that coupé? It must have cost a fortune.'

'And her blouse—it looked as if it was made by Ossie Clark . . .'

'So what was she doing with a passenger like that?' The amusement began to die out of his face. 'I hope he hasn't got important friends. I was quite rude to him this morning—told him to push off.'

Clarissa had nothing like that with which to reproach herself. She was more intrigued by the personal angle. What possible relationship could there be between that girl and the man from the building site? Everything about her bespoke money and chic—and moreover there was nothing to imply the eccentric, the bohemian, who might give a lift to a stranded workman. In any case, the car had come out of the underground car park, which meant that these two must have gone together on foot and got into the car—no question there of seeing some-one by the roadside trying to thumb a lift.

Incomprehensible, the whole thing.

Because she could see it rather worried Jean-Louis, she set herself to question him about the strange 'harbour-bar' she could see jutting out into the lake about a quarter of a mile away. He explained that it was

22

a swimming area, and suggested they should go back to her apartment for a swimsuit.

'No, no, I've no energy for swimming. Don't forget I spent all yesterday packing up and travelling, while last night I only got about three hours' sleep. No, no, a gentle stroll in the sun is much more in my line at the moment.'

They spent the morning ambling along the lake shore. About eleven-thirty she recalled that she ought to do some shopping for provisions, so they left the tree-lined Quai du Mont Blanc and took a trolleybus back to the *marché*. Here she bought bread and fruit and cold meat, and by then it was midday.

'I could offer you lunch,' she remarked, indicating her purchases, 'if you'd care to come back to the apartment?'

'Much as I'd love to, I'm afraid I must refuse. I must get home and start work on those pictures.'

'Where is "home", by the way? What part of Geneva do you live?'

'Actually my studio is in Lausanne—'

'Good gracious, Jean-Louis, I'd no idea! You've got quite a drive back—'

'No, no, it's only a few miles along the lake. I'll be home within the hour. But I really think I ought to go now, because if the proofs don't look too good when I run them off tonight, I can come back tomorrow and take some more shots. So if you don't mind I'll say no to lunch today. But—' and he smiled—'there will be other days. May I ring you?'

'I don't even know if there's a phone at the apartment,' she admitted, a little astounded that since arriving last night she'd only spent one waking hour in her new home and learned almost nothing about its amenities.

'I'll ring you at Entreprise Pagel on Monday.'

'I'll look forward to that.'

He took her hand, and she thought it was for the usual formal handshake. But to her surprise he raised it to his lips. '*A bientôt*,' he murmured.

She made her way home up the steep lane reflecting that so far life in Geneva had proved very eventful. For lunch she made herself a snack, then settled down to listen to the news programme on Radio Romande. But drowsiness overcame her, and when she opened her eyes again it was six o'clock—she'd been catching up on the sleep she lost last night.

Determined not to spend her first evening indoors and half asleep, she washed and changed. Ten minutes later she was tapping at the *concièrge*'s door to inquire if Madame Lallais could recommend a good restaurant for dinner. The old lady raised her eyebrows.

'Doesn't the young man know the restaurants of Geneva?'

'The young man? Oh, Jean-Louis! He's gone home to Lausanne.'

'You're going out alone?'

'Certainly. Why not?'

'Oh, well, these days, I suppose ... In my young days a lady did not go out in the evening without an escort.'

'Really, Madame Lallais, I've no choice. I haven't *got* an escort!'

'You could stay at home,' Madame said rather sternly.

'Alone? On my first evening in Geneva?'

'Ah, yes. I see.' Madame relented. 'Come then and have dinner with me. I have a very good *longeole* and we could make a dessert—'

'Thank you, Madame Lallais,' Clarissa put in hastily, 'but I would very much like to try a restaurant and taste a genuine *fondue*. You do understand?'

'Ah, young people, young people ... Well, *mademoiselle*, I can recommend the Baronne, which is in the Rue Vervain. The food is excellent there. Or L'Ours de Berne—there's folk-music there on Saturday nights, and you won't come to any harm because they take the tourists there.'

'Thank you! Where is L'Ours de Berne?'

'You'd better take a taxi. I'll ring for one.' She went indoors, and to pass the time until the taxi came Clarissa sauntered out into the lane.

The men from the building site further up were getting ready go home. In the background of her attention

24

she'd heard the machinery cease to throb and now one or two workers puttered away on the little '*motos*' she'd seen everywhere today. A little Fiat van pulled out from the kerb and drove off—leaving visible to her startled gaze the handsome dark blue Lamborghini she'd seen at the lake car park. It was parked and unoccupied. She glanced about for the girl in the pink silk shirt, but she was nowhere to be seen.

Two men came out of the gates of the building site, deep in conversation. One she didn't know, but she had no difficulty in recognising the other. He was bending his head to listen to his colleague, nodding as if in agreement, and then raising his hand in farewell as the shorter man walked briskly away.

Turning, he saw Clarissa. Only a few yards of pavement separated them. For a moment she thought he was going to disregard her, but after a fractional hesitation he came up.

'So we meet again,' he said. His glance took in her rather elegant dress of dark brown cotton. 'Off for another night's amusement?'

'Another? I do wish I could make it clear to you—! I was *not* on my way home from a night on the tiles when you saw me this morning. That was my dressing-gown I had on.' She bit her lip: why on earth was she explaining? What could it possibly matter if he had misunderstood?

'Do you often come out into the street in a dressing-gown?'

'Only when I'm startled awake at the crack of dawn! I shall complain to Monsieur Pagel about it.'

He looked taken aback. 'Monsieur Pagel?'

'Yes,' she went on, pleased to see she'd made an impression on him at last. She hadn't the slightest intention of mentioning the matter to Monsieur Pagel—from his reputation he scarcely seemed the sort of employer she could trouble with a small matter of disturbed sleep. But the threat certainly seemed to have an effect on him. 'It so happens that I arrived from England late last night to take up employment in Monsieur Pagel's office, so on Monday I shall tell him how inconsiderate you were, and you can rest assured you'll hear more on that score.'

'You'll really report me to him?'

'I certainly shall!'

'Don't you think that's rather a . . .' He paused, and then to her astonishment brought out in English the word . . . 'sneak thing to do?'

'You speak English?' she said in surprise.

'A little. We building workers, we go all over the world. And so—here you are on your first evening in Geneva?'

She nodded.

'And you are going out to dinner. With the young cameraman?' His hand sketched the equipment hanging round Jean-Louis' neck. 'He's very quick to follow up an advantage, that one!'

'I can't see that it's any business of yours,' she said with a studied coldness of manner. 'Good evening to you.'

Her taxi had just drawn up at the door of the block. She went quickly to it and got in. As she was driven away she glanced back to see the tall man staring after her.

She had a good meal and a pleasant evening but came home early, knowing that fatigue was about to catch up with her again. As she prepared for bed she could hear in her mind the echo of the song the folk-group had been singing as she left:

> Leave these fields and fountains,
> Seek out some hidden grove,
> Climb to the highest mountain,
> Wherever you go, you'll find love!

The lilting refrain seemed to haunt her dreams.

She spent Sunday very quietly, so that on Monday morning she was up bright and early to make her way to the headquarters of Entreprise Pagel, an imposing building she had already spied out in the Rue Versonnex. When she presented herself to the receptionist she was greeted with some deference: 'Monsieur Pagel is expecting you. Please follow the page-boy.'

Rather surprised, she did as she was bid. Nothing had led her to expect that the terrible Roland Pagel would bother to welcome her personally. She was taken up in an express lift to the penthouse level, conducted to an ante-room, and left in the care of a middle-aged secretary who beckoned her to sit down and wait.

Some minutes passed. The secretary had said nothing beyond good morning. The atmosphere was not welcoming: in fact quite the reverse. Clarissa began to feel terribly nervous.

A buzzer sounded on the secretary's desk. She flicked the intercom switch. '*M'sieur?*'

'Send her in,' said a voice, distorted and depersonalised by the microphone.

The secretary waved her towards the finely panelled door of the inner office. By now quite intimidated, Clarissa tapped gently and went in.

Sitting at a big desk behind an array of telephones was the tall man whom Clarissa had seen at five o'clock on Saturday morning driving a dump-truck. Instead of a dusty blue shirt and a safety helmet he was now wearing a light grey suit of very fine worsted. His hands rested on the blotter in front of him, loosely clasped. He looked entirely at home.

'Now, Mademoiselle Oakley,' he said, 'I believe you have a complaint to make to me about a lack of consideration shown to you on Saturday?'

CHAPTER II

There was only one thought in Clarissa's head: if she'd studied for a twelvemonth to find a way of beginning badly at Entreprise Pagel, she couldn't have done better.

Dumbstruck, she stared at her employer. He for his part was surveying her with grim amusement. 'What's the matter?' he inquired in English 'Cat got your tongue?'

'I ... I ...' On the way to the office she had re-

hearsed a few polite phrases to use should good luck
cause her path to cross Monsieur Pagel's. 'I appreciate
this chance to work in Switzerland.' And, 'You can be
sure I'll work hard.' None of them seemed to fit the
present situation. She burst out: 'You might have told
me who you were!'

'Why should I? I had no reason to think my name
would mean a thing to you, until you yourself brought it
into the conversation.'

'You could have told me *then*.'

'If you remember, you went hurrying away to keep
your date with Monsieur Blech. You had a pleasant
evening, I trust?'

'Yes, thank you.' Nothing would have induced her to
say that she had not spent Saturday evening with Jean-
Louis but had dined alone and been in bed and asleep
at ten-fifteen.

'Sunday, too, was entertaining?'

'Equally so.'

'To the extent that you've forgotten the complaint you
intended to make?'

'Well, I ... that is, there was never any real intention ...'

'You were making a threat you had no intention of
carrying out, I gather.'

'It was just that I thought you—'

'Please go on.'

'I thought you'd be more considerate about all that
noise if you knew I ... might report it. Of course I see
now you must have been laughing up your sleeve all the
time.'

'Up my sleeve?' he repeated, faintly puzzled.

'It's an English idiom. It means "secretly".'

'Ah yes. You are quite right. I got quite a lot of
amusement out of your behaviour.'

She coloured. 'Don't you think that was rather a ...
sneak thing to do?'

For one awful moment he looked astounded at having
his own words repeated back to him. Then, unexpectedly, he threw back his head and laughed.

Clarissa suddenly went quite weak with relief. That

impulse of retaliation, which had made her quote his own phrase, could easily have ended with her dismissal. She couldn't understand her own reaction; normally she had far too much good sense to do anything that would damage her career prospects. What was it about this man that made her hackles rise?

Well, she answered herself, that's easy—the same thing that's caused one secretary after another to give notice or get thrown out—his bad manners. But she was going to have to put up with them if she wanted to stay in Switzerland.

'Mademoiselle Oakley,' he remarked in French, shaking his head, 'it is impossible *not* to be amused by you. Perhaps I should be grateful—you've taken my mind off one or two business problems and given me some light relief.' He paused. 'As to the noise on the building site, I'm afraid you will have to endure it. While the summer weather is here we must put in all the hours we can. You'll appreciate, I'm sure, that it's difficult to work once six feet of snow has fallen.'

'Yes, but—'

'But what?'

'Don't people object? I'd have thought it was bad public relations for Pagel's.'

The cool grey-green eyes narrowed. 'What time did you get up this morning, *mademoiselle*, in order to be punctual at the office?'

'Seven o'clock, sir.'

'You were lucky. I was up at five-thirty, and so were a great many of my countrymen. It's something you will just have to get used to, Miss Oakley—we rise early, we start work early, and we expect men on a construction site to be there and making a noise. I quite admit—' he held up a hand as she was about to speak— 'that on Saturday I was somewhat in advance of the usual starting time. That was because I knew your friend Blech was going to be there before the construction team, to take some publicity photographs. I wanted to be sure that everything was safe for him—as you say, it would be bad public relations for Pagel's if he had brought a pile of scaffolding down on top of him.'

'I see. I ... I'm sorry. I didn't understand.'

'I accept your apology.'

Clarissa had an odd feeling that now it was his turn to apologise, for having made a fool of her. But of course he didn't.

Instead he said curtly: 'That will be all. Madame Gebermann will give you your instructions. Good morning.'

'Good morning, Monsieur Pagel.'

As she closed the door softly behind her the middle-aged secretary rose to greet her again. There was no mistaking the gleam of interest, quickly hidden, which showed in her eyes.

'Monsieur Pagel said I was to get my instructions from Madame Gebermann . . . ?'

'I am Madame Gebermann.' She offered her hand, which Clarissa shook formally. It struck her that Madame Gebermann hadn't shaken hands with her when she first appeared; presumably it was so unusual for Monsieur Pagel to summon a new employee to his presence that she'd been waiting to see whether Clarissa was to be fired before she ever started work.

She led the way out of her office and along a lushly-carpeted passage. From the big windows Clarissa saw a vista of roof tops and then the lake glinting in restless swathes of silver and gold under a cloud-flecked but sunny sky. They went into a room where another girl was at work on a dictaphone. Madame Gebermann introduced her as Babette Georgeot but scarcely gave time for the required formal handshake before ushering Clarissa to a desk on the other side of the room.

It was well equipped, with a splendid electric type-writer and the latest in desk-filing equipment. But Clarissa's heart sank at the pile of work in the 'In' tray.

'Your duties,' Madame Gebermann explained, 'are concerned entirely with correspondence in the English language. Since your predecessor left rather ... suddenly, and we have for some days been without an English-language secretary, I have taken dictation from Monsieur Pagel. You will be so good as to type it up as quickly as you can and get the letters ready for signature.'

'Yes, Madame Gebermann.'

'When you have done, let us say, six of them, please bring them to me. I will take them in for Monsieur Pagel to sign along with any other correspondence.'

'Yes, Madame Gebermann.'

'You and Mademoiselle Georgeot can make your own arrangements about who is to go to lunch first. I myself go at noon. One or other of you must be here while I am out.'

'Yes, Madame Gebermann.'

The other woman smiled suddenly. 'I hope you'll be able to read my shorthand,' she remarked. 'Taking note in a language other than one's own is always a little awkward, and some of my outlines may puzzle you. If so, please don't hesitate to ask.'

'Thank you, *madame*.'

'Very well. I'll leave you in Mademoiselle Georgeot's capable hands.'

When she had gone the other girl leaned back and took of her earpiece. 'Hello,' she said. 'I hear you were marched into the lion's den as soon as you arrived.'

'Y-yes.' Clarissa met her glance rather warily, but there was so much good-humoured interest in the blue eyes that she began to relax.

'What happened? Was he warning you you'd have to do better than Jenny?'

'No, he just wanted to know whether . . . whether I had any complaints.'

'Any complaints? But you've only just arrived! How could you have—?'

'Did Jenny have this desk?' Clarissa interrupted, not at all willing to make explanations.

'Yes, for the short time she was here. How do you think *you'll* like it here, now you've met him?'

'I shall be all right,' said Clarissa with determination. 'He doesn't scare *me*.'

Mademoiselle Georgeot's expression showed a certain amount of incredulity at that remark, but she began a discussion about the office routine. It was agreed that since Clarissa wanted to make some inroads on the pile of work on her desk, she should go to lunch late; 'late' meant one o'clock, which to Clarissa seemed if anything rather early since in London she was accustomed to going at one-fifteen. But she soon discovered that the Genevais lunch early because they breakfast early, and to turn up at a restaurant much after one meant that the place was emptying.

'Phone calls will be put through to this office if Madame Gebermann is out,' Mademoiselle Georgeot explained. 'Neither of us two is required to do anything except take a message and say Madame Gebermann will attend to it as soon as she returns. Get it?'

'Yes, I understand.' Clarissa sighed. 'That's a bit ... limiting, isn't it?'

'It's a great blessing! There's quite enough to do without trying to handle the phone, *mademoiselle*.'

Privately Clarissa considered that to be cooped up all day typing letters and in the company of a girl who insisted on being addressed as '*mademoiselle*' was rather dull. Back home the two of them would have been on first-name terms at once. But she had known that things were much more formal here, so she had no cause for complaint—and in fact in a day or two she and the plump, blue-eyed Babette were almost like sisters.

For today, however, all was to be strictly according to etiquette. Babette stopped work at noon, switched off her machine, smoothed her dark skirt over her rather ample hips, and announced that she was going. 'You'll be all right, Mademoiselle Oakley?'

'Quite all right, thank you, *mademoiselle*.'

'*À bientôt, mademoiselle*.'

Clarissa smiled an absent-minded farewell and went back to the notebook. '. . . But feel that the basic lay-out . . .' Or was it 'basement layout'? She read to the end of the letter, decided that a discussion of future extensions to a college was more likely to be concerned with basic layout than the basement, and began to type.

Many times she had to stop to make decisions of this kind. It wasn't the fault of Madame Gebermann's shorthand, simply that she was unfamiliar with the turn of speech of the man who had dictated the letter. And he, of course, had been dictating in a language not his own. He spoke it well, but now and again there were problems. What, for instance, could he mean by 'off the rack'? 'I can see no solution off the rack.' 'I can see no solution of the rack,' with only one 'f'—? Even then it didn't seem to make much sense.

The telephone rang. Startled, Clarissa turned her head. It rang again. 'Go on, you idiot,' she said, 'answer it.' Gingerly she picked it up. 'Entreprise Pagel,' she said.

'Good heavens, I know it's Entreprise Pagel,' said an annoyed voice in French. 'I asked to be put through to Roland Pagel.' She sounded as if it was a frequent request.

'Oh ... I see ... I'm sorry, his personal secretary is at lunch. May I take a message?'

'I don't want to speak to his secretary, I want to speak to Monsieur Pagel. Put me through at once!'

'I'm sorry, *mademoiselle*, but I was instructed by Madame Gebermann—'

The annoyed voice was heard to mutter something that sounded like 'that stupid old guard-dog!' 'Never mind what she instructed. Monsieur Pagel is expecting my call. Put me through, please.'

'I can't, *mademoiselle*. I—'

'What do you mean, you can't? Do as you're told!'

'But I don't know *how*, *mademoiselle*,' Clarissa confessed. 'This is just an ordinary telephone, so I could only put you back to the switchboard—'

'Heaven preserve me! What are you, an imbecile? What does Gebermann do when she puts a call through to Roland?'

'I've no idea, *mademoiselle*. I only started work here four hours ago.' Clarissa paused. An angry silence at the other end greeted her information. 'May I take a message?' she inquired. 'I really think it would be best, because if I put you back to the switchboard they would presumably put you back to Madame Gebermann's extension, and *her* calls are being transferred here—'

'Spare me the telephone engineering! Where is "here", anyway? Who are you?'

'I work in Monsieur Pagel's office—'

'No, you don't. Oh, I see—you're the new English girl. I knew I'd never heard your voice before. Very well, you'd better take a message. My name is Masagram—have you got that?' She spelt it, slowly and distinctly, as if addressing a three-year-old. 'Tell Monsieur Pagel to let me know whether or not he's coming to the Chaval reception. If he is, I want him to—No, never mind. Just ask him to ring me. He knows my number.'

'Yes, *mademoiselle*,' murmured Clarissa, but before she'd finished saying it the phone was put down at the other end.

A very cross caller, Clarissa thought. Somehow she was certain that the voice belonged to the girl she'd seen on Saturday, the girl driving the big Lamborghini, the girl in the beautiful silk shirt. The authoritative manner, the expectation of obedience—these somehow matched the impression Clarissa had received, even in that brief glimpse, of a woman of drive and ability. Try as she might, she could not summon up any remembrance of her features. *That* was odd. Generally Clarissa was observant of other women.

Could it be that all her attention had been on Roland Pagel, sitting in the passenger seat?

Well, why not? At that time she had still thought he was a dump-truck driver, and you had to admit that seeing a dump-truck driver in a millionaire-type car was unusual.

Giving herself a little shake, she returned to Madame Gebermann's shorthand. 'I can see no solution of the rack, but if you let me have your thoughts on this ...' It still didn't seem right. She picked up the notebook and took it to the window, hoping that by holding the page to the light she might see some angle or emphasis in the outline that she'd missed. But it still looked the same—neat, painstaking, not as fluid as her own would have been, and of course she would have used the short-form for some of the phrases ...

Her eyes wandered past the page to the view outside. A seagull was floating on motionless wings above the roofs, his white feathers gleaming as he swayed and tilted in the air current. Lucky you, she thought—free to float above the lake, to feel the sun on your back and the breeze against your weight. How lovely to be like him . . .

Beyond him was the sparkle of Lake Geneva and beyond again, the mountains. On the peaks the snow was as white as the gull's breast-feathers. To be up there, where it was cold and clear and silent—how would she like that? She knew nothing about mountains, but that cold austere glint seemed to call to her.

What had the folk-group sung?

> Climb to the highest mountain,
> Wherever you go, you'll find love . . .

She hummed it to herself, hearing the soft chords of the guitar accompaniment and the harmony of the voices.

> Do you see the snow-slope shining
> Up there on that frowning peak . . .

'Where did you learn that?' said a voice from the doorway.

She whirled. Her employer was standing there, his jacket over his arm. 'I'm sorry, sir,' she faltered. 'Is there something you want?'

'Not a thing.' He sauntered into the doorway. 'How do you come to know "*Voyez -vous la neige*"?'

'I heard it sung by a folk-music quartet on Saturday evening, at L'Ours de Berne.'

'Really?' He gave a little frown. 'I would hardly have expected Jean-Louis Blech to take you to hear Swiss folk-songs.'

'Nevertheless that was where I heard it.'

'It's from my district—it's a song from the Vaud. My mother used to—' He broke off. 'Well, I'm happy to know that you're taking an interest in our traditions, but it doesn't explain why you're gazing dreamily out of the window during working hours!'

It was a great comfort to know that she had a complete answer to that. 'I was examining this shorthand outline, Monsieur Pagel. I'm not sure I'm transcribing it correctly.'

'Are you going to tell me now that your shorthand is inadequate? If so I'll have something to say to the London branch. They understood my requirements.'

Kindling, Clarissa held the notebook out to him. 'Perhaps you could read it for me, sir?'

She knew it would anger him, and felt no surprise—only a cold little triumph—when his face darkened. 'My work is construction engineering, not stenography—'

'Exactly. And mine is stenography, not construction engineering. I can read the outline, and in fact I could type the phrase into the letter and leave it to you to say whether it's right or wrong. Only I happen to take a pride in my work, and this doesn't seem to me to make good sense.'

They were standing facing each other a few feet apart, the notebook held out like a challenge between them. There was a long moment of antagonism. Then he gave himself a little shake and said brusquely: 'Read it to me.'

She let her eyes run over the page. Truth to tell, she was glad not to have to meet his gaze any more. It was as cold as the snows on the mountaintops over there . . .

' "I can see no solution of the rack",' she read, ' "but if you will let me have your thoughts on this . . . " '

He folded his arms across his folded jacket and looked thoughtful. 'What's wrong with it?'

'There's no mention of a rack anywhere else in the letter, Monsieur Pagel.'

'No? It's some days since I dictated it. Read me what goes before.'

She obeyed, and when she came to the problem sentence he snapped his fingers in understanding. '*C'est ça*. I remember. I was telling Johnson that I could see no solution *off* the rack.'

'Off what rack?' Clarissa asked, baffled.

'Off the rack . . . the rack!' He hoisted his jacket by its hanging-loop. 'The rack from which one buys clothes *prêt-à-porter*—ready-made!'

36

Light dawned. 'Off the *peg!*'

'*Comment?*'

'Off the peg. Not off the rack.'

'Wait a moment,' said Monsieur Pagel, raising his jacket again. 'One goes into a restaurant and one hangs one's coat on a rack. Yes or no?' He was demonstrating as he spoke.

'Quite correct. But on the rack there are pegs, and it is on the peg'—Clarissa hooked her finger under the jacket-loop—'that one hangs the coat.'

'Really?'

'And one buys clothes off the peg.'

'But that doesn't seem quite logical because—'

'Don't expect me to explain the logic of the English language,' Clarissa said ruefully, surrendering his jacket to him again. 'All I can tell you is that ready-made solutions are solutions "off the peg".'

'I see. Very well.' A pause. 'Thank you for correcting the mistake. If you had not, the letter would have gone out as it stood and our friend Basil Johnson would have wondered what I was talking about. Bad for public relations, eh?'

Clarissa gave him a smile of acquiescence. She didn't like to appear too wholehearted in her agreement because that would have been tantamount to saying she had saved him from looking foolish. To change the subject she went to her desk where she retrieved the telephone-message pad.

'A Mademoiselle Masagram called, sir. She wants you to ring her.'

Did she only imagine it, or did his mood of relaxation change?

'Did she say why?'

'She mentioned something about the hotel chain—the one for whom you're building—' she was seeking a recollection of the name. 'Oh yes—Chaval! It was something about Chaval.'

He turned towards the door, muttering to himself. She thought she caught the word 'trouble'.

'I don't think it's anything like that, sir,' she volunteered. 'I think she was inviting you to a reception.'

He stopped to give her a cold smile. 'My dear Miss Oakley, when the Public Relations Director of a firm as big as Chaval asks you to a reception, you can be almost sure it's to pressure you into yet more troubles than you have already. Simone Masagram never does anything without a motive—in fact, several motives.'

'Oh, I see. I rather got the impression it was a personal call.'

'That too,' he said as he went out.

Clarissa had no idea why his reply should make her feel vaguely despondent.

That evening she was to meet Jean-Louis for a drink on the way home from the office; he had rung while she was at lunch, so that Babette had taken a message for her. The rendezvous was a hotel not far from the great plume of water that rose into the evening sky from the *Jetée des Eaux Vives*. Babette had told her it was easy to find— all she had to do was take a trolleybus.

But what she hadn't said was which bus stop to find the bus. Clarissa walked to the end of the Rue du Rhône, but once there stood hesitating, watching the groups at the various boarding points. Traffic was moving gently from the Rue Versonnex, but she wasn't paying attention until short, repeated taps on a car horn made her turn.

It was the dark blue Lamborghini. Roland Pagel was at the wheel.

'Where are you heading?' he called.

'Avenue William Favre.'

'Hop in, I'll take you.'

Quite overwhelmed, she did as she was bid. The soft white leather of the seats seemed to invite her to relax, and after a day which had taken a great deal out of her she sighed with pleasure.

'What a beautiful car,' she said.

'You like it? I must admit cars are my one weakness.'

'You mean this is your car?'

He spared a glance before giving full attention to picking his way into the main traffic streams. 'Why else do you think I'm driving it?'

She made an apologetic sound. 'It's only that when I

saw you on Saturday . . .'

'Ah yes. Simone had asked for a chance to try it out. Cars are a weakness of hers too.'

She should have thought that out for herself. No Press Relations Director, however well paid, could afford a car like this.

'I hope I'm not taking you out of your way, Monsieur Pagel,' she murmured.

'It's no trouble. I have an appointment later, but there's plenty of time. You were quite right, by the way —it *was* an invitation to a reception.' She saw him give a wry smile. 'I shall turn up as late as I possibly can.'

'Perhaps it will be fun when you get there.'

'Oh, perhaps. Perhaps the River Rhône will begin to flow backwards.'

'Don't you like parties?'

'Not much. I take it you do?'

'I must admit I do.'

'Is that where you're going now? To a party?'

'Oh no, sir—it's just to meet a friend . . .'

He didn't ask who the friend was. After a little he began to ask if she liked the office, if the apartment provided by Entreprise Pagel was comfortable. She replied politely. Quite soon she saw a street nameboard: Avenue William Favre. 'We're here,' she remarked.

'Where are you meeting your friend?'

'The Hotel Prélude.'

'Ah. You won't find anything as old-fashioned as a folk-singer there. It goes in for science-fiction décor and music from electronic tapes.'

'Oh dear.'

'Shall I drive you home instead?' he inquired.

'No, Jean-Louis will be waiting—' She broke off, unwilling to say anything more about Jean-Louis for fear of giving a wrong impression.

'Very well. Here we are.' He drew up outside a portico in black marble embellished with thunderbolts in crystal and bronze. He leaned over to open the door so that she could get out, which she did hastily. 'If you like parties,' he said, touching her wrist as she was moving away, 'I hope you'll enjoy our thirty-first.'

She came back. 'I'm sorry?'

'The eve of our national day. You know August the first is the day we commemorate the Swiss alliance?'

'Oh yes—I read a little about it before I came.'

'Good for you. But perhaps you didn't know that we have Pernods and parties on the day before. Entreprise Pagel does its share of celebrating—on the evening of the day before, we give a party for all our staff.'

'That sounds fun. I'll look forward to it.'

He smiled and took his hand away. 'Enjoy your futuristic evening.'

'Thank you. I hope your reception is more enjoyable than you expect.'

He nodded and put the car in gear. When she reached the top of the shallow steps at the hotel entrance she looked back, but the Lamborghini was already out of sight.

She was too early. Jean-Louis was nowhere to be seen. But the bar of the hotel was very quiet, very respectable. She settled at a table with a welcome glass of iced lemon and mineral water; she found the warmth of the lake shores made her continually thirsty. The barman brought her the newspaper. Soft, rather eerie music made a cool background.

When Jean-Louis arrived he came not from outside but from the manager's office. 'Have I kept you waiting? I'm so sorry, Clarissa—I've been working here all day—pictures for their advertising brochure.' He subsided beside her on the leather bench. '*What* a time I've had! This black marble they've used is very smart, of course, but it tends to look gloomy on the page.'

Clarissa listened sympathetically to his problems, but with only half her mind. It was difficult to say where the other half was; she kept constructing pictures of a very smart cocktail party, and then scrapping them because only two of those present had any reality—Roland Pagel and Simone Masagram.

She became aware, from the upward tone, that Jean-Louis had just asked a question. 'What did you say, Jean-Louis? I'm sorry, I was miles away.'

'What were you thinking about?'

'Oh, nothing, really—'

'Tell me. Was it about the job? How did it go, your first day?'

'Not bad. Some shocks, some good things.'

'Shocks?' Jean-Louis beckoned the barman to bring him *trois decis de blancs* by holding up three fingers and nodding towards the bunch of white grapes depicted symbolically on the porcelain tiles shading the lights. 'Who's been giving you shocks?'

'Monsieur Pagel, chiefly.'

He looked sympathetic. 'Yes, you said he was an old ogre. What a shame, my poor little girl!'

'He's not so very old, Jean-Louis. In fact . . .'

'What?'

'Remember the man at the building site on Saturday morning?'

'The one I ordered off? Yes, what about him?'

'That's Roland Pagel.'

Jean-Louis' jaw dropped. A look of utter horror washed over his thin face. 'Y-you're joking!' he stammered.

'No, it's quite true. Remember we saw him being driven along the lakeside in a gorgeous car? Well, it's *his* car. The girl who was driving had begged for a chance to try it out.'

'But . . . but . . . he had a protective helmet on . . .'

'Oh yes. A man as rich as that can be eccentric if he likes.'

'*Bon dieu*,' groaned Jean-Louis. 'And I was so *rude* to him!'

Clarissa surprised herself by giving a little chuckle. 'I was pretty rude to him too. But as a matter of fact . . .'

'What?'

'He doesn't seem to be the type who holds a grudge. In fact, he invited me to a party.'

The waiter arrived with the measure of wine in a handsome little carafe. Jean-Louis kept silent while it was poured into the glass. When they were alone again he said with studied calmness, 'Now, Clarissa, have the goodness to explain what happened.'

41

'I told you. In the course of conversation I'd mentioned I like folk music, so he said he hoped I'd enjoy the party on the thirty-first. It's a sort of office party, I take it. He told me about it while he was giving me a lift in that fabulous car.'

His eyes snapped with delight. 'Clarissa! He's taken a fancy to you!'

Clarissa frowned. She felt her cheeks go hot. 'Don't talk nonsense.'

'But he has! Gives you a lift, invites you to a party—'

'Only an office party. Everybody will be there—the doorman, the lift attendant—'

'Don't be naïve, Clarissa. You admit yourself that by all the usual reckoning he ought to have been annoyed with you, but no—he makes a fuss of you.' He took a sip of his wine, looking thoughtful. 'I believe it isn't unusual. I've heard some gossip about him—some story or other—I can't remember what, but I know it was about some affair he'd had . . .'

'Jean-Louis! That's quite enough!'

'What's the matter?' He was surprised, and perhaps with reason. 'You're not carrying loyalty to the point where you think your employer has no faults?'

'Of course not, but all the same I don't think I want to hear about his private affairs.'

'But my dear girl, you ought to know, surely? If he's going to start taking an interest in you?'

'*Jean-Louis!*' She felt as if the skin of her cheeks was on fire. His matter-of-fact way of discussing such a thing was almost as embarrassing as what he was discussing. 'I've had about ten or fifteen minutes' conversation with Monsieur Pagel. It's absurd to read anything more into it than common politeness.'

'I bet he's not "polite" in that way to many people. Didn't you tell me that you got this job because so many other girls couldn't stand up to his authoritarian ways?'

Her silence admitted the truth of it. After a moment Jean-Louis continued: 'If anything comes of it, put in a good word for me, Clarissa.'

'Oh, honestly, I can't imagine . . .'

'Explain that I didn't mean what I said on Saturday

42

morning.'

'And didn't you?'

'Of course I did—but I thought he was a truck-driver then!' To do him justice, Jean-Louis grinned at his own duplicity. 'If I'd had the slightest idea he was a millionaire playing Cinderella, I would never have spoken to him in that tone of voice.'

'Oh . . . Jean-Louis . . .'

'What's the matter? Does it shock you because I feel more respect for Roland Pagel than for some nonentity on a building site? Come, come, Clarissa—my reaction is no different from your own. You wouldn't have gone marching down from your apartment at dawn on Saturday morning to read a lecture to Roland Pagel.'

She had to agree that this was so. 'But all the same . . .'

'What?'

'I don't know.' She couldn't quite bring herself to express her feelings. She'd thought that Jean-Louis felt some attraction towards her, yet now he was prepared to hand her over, lock, stock and barrel to the rich Monsieur Pagel. And to make a little advantage for himself out of the transaction. She said in a rather flat voice: 'I shouldn't build any hopes on my having influence with Monsieur Pagel.'

'But if he's decided to . . . er . . . take an interest in you?'

'Don't be absurd, Jean-Louis. He hasn't decided anything of the kind.'

'It *could* happen,' he urged. 'You're pretty in your quiet way—like a little brown bird—'

'Oh, do be sensible! Have you forgotten the girl who was with him on Saturday? From what I imagine, she's not likely to let him "take an interest" in anyone but herself. And besides . . .'

'What?'

I'm not the kind of girl who lets her employer 'take an interest' in her—not in that way. Those were the words that beat out their rhythm behind her brow. But she left them unsaid. It would be too difficult to explain it all to Jean-Louis: the innate sense of honour that

43

weighed actions and intentions against some golden scruple, the ambition that urged her always to make her way on merit only, not on emotional blackmail or the politics of office romance.

It was too complex to explain even to another woman; to get it across to a man, and such a man as Jean-Louis, was impossible. Clarissa was not an innocent; she saw what went on in the world around her with clear eyes. But her own standards were different. She didn't want to fall in love, nor to pretend to fall in love: she wanted to be a success, and to do that she had to stay untrammelled by romantic involvement. Friendship, yes; passion, no. That was her plan.

But she answered Jean-Louis' inquiry with a shrug, and a little while later remarked that it was time to go home. He made no demur; he had film to develop, and since she didn't seem inclined to talk about the great and important Roland Pagel, there was no more to be gained for the present.

At the office a mounting excitement heralded the coming of the National Day. Flags and banners appeared in the streets—the white cross on red that betokened Switzerland, and the heraldic emblems of the cantons. Geneva's banner was very beautiful, a shield bearing a golden key symbolising the Cathedral and a half-eagle on its yellow ground for the days when, a thousand years ago, it was part of the German Empire. But Clarissa noticed that when Monsieur Pagel, like many others, took to wearing a little enamelled badge, his was green and white with the words '*Liberté et Patrie*'— 'Liberty and my Homeland.'

'That's the arms of Vaud Canton, isn't it?' she inquired of Babette.

'Yes, quite right. But how did you know that?'

'He told me he—that is, I heard he came from the Vaud.'

'I suppose he does, otherwise he wouldn't wear the badge.'

'It's rather . . .'

'What?'

'I don't know exactly . . . charming, artless . . . I

44

wouldn't have thought Monsieur Pagel was the sort of man to feel an uncomplicated patriotism.'

Babette wrinkled her nose and laughed. 'I can give you an uncomplicated explanation,' she remarked. 'It's good business to show a little patriotism at a time like this!'

Clarissa had to admit to herself that Babette was probably right. She gave herself a little shake—why on earth was she inventing complimentary reasons for Monsieur Pagel's actions? All the same, she was unreasonably pleased next day when little desk flags were handed out, to find that hers was the green and white of the Vaud.

On the thirty-first the office closed at noon. Everyone went home to put on their best clothes and return at four for the party. For this purpose the cafeteria had been transformed into an Alpine kitchen, with all sorts of cold meats and salads set out on wooden platters, hot sausages on the griddle, and flagons of wine lined up on a stone bench.

The place was crowded, but it soon became clear to Clarissa that the crowd divided into three main groups—the serious eaters who stayed near the buffet, the merrymakers who were dancing or trying their hand at party games, and the 'important' people. The 'important' people didn't eat much, either because they thought it beneath their dignity or intended to have dinner in a couple of hours' time; they stood about in knots of three or four, talking. Clarissa noticed that most of the young executives had enrolled themselves in the ranks of the 'important' people, and the women with them—wives, fiancées—were very elegant.

Outshining all of them, though, was Simone Masagram. She had come in a trouser suit of plain white silk, above which her fine tanned skin gleamed like Peruvian gold. She wore no jewellery except baroque pearls in her ears, whose exquisite smallness was left uncovered by her short hairstyle.

Covertly Clarissa studied her. She certainly wasn't beautiful—no more so than Clarissa herself. But by superb grooming and an unerring instinct for dramatic simplicity, she made herself unforgettable.

In a way she was what Clarissa wanted to be. She held down a difficult, demanding job which brought her both prestige and a more-than-adequate salary. She had used her intelligence to lift herself out of the ordinary. Yet, strange to say, Clarissa didn't feel any great urge to admire her.

Mademoiselle Masagram was part of a group which included Roland Pagel and some of the chief members of his staff, together with their guests. Among these Clarissa noted two men who were obviously father and son, if facial resemblance was any guide. The elder was distinguished to look at, his thinning grey hair brushed back rather severely and his austere features outlined by a beautifully trimmed grey beard. The younger man had the same rather severe features, but softened by a look of anxiety, almost of insecurity. He didn't appear to be enjoying himself half as much as his father, who was talking with animation.

Some moments later the group had moved and re-formed slightly, in the way that such things happen at a party. Clarissa saw that the young man had somehow been shouldered out to the edge of the circle; he stood for a moment trying to listen to what was being said, but when an outburst of laughter greeted a joke he hadn't caught, he looked down unhappily at his glass of wine, hunched into himself a little, then turned away.

An impulse of sympathy took Clarissa towards him. She too was something of an outsider at this celebration. 'Can I get you another drink?' she inquired.

'Er . . . no, thank you . . . I . . . don't drink much.'— There was a hesitation in his speech which might turn into a stammer in times of stress.

'Some food, then? The smoked ham is very good.'

'Well . . . perhaps.' He let her take his arm to guide him to the buffet. 'You're English, aren't you?'

'Yes, I attend to the English correspondence for Monsieur Pagel. My name is Clarissa Oakley.'

'Edouard Masagram,' he announced, offering his hand.

'Masagram?' She glanced back towards the group he
46

had left.

'Simone is my sister,' he explained.

'And the gentleman with the beard?'

'That's Papa. Could you tell he was a relative?'

'Of course. The resemblance is very marked.'

'In looks only,' he said, but in a sort of mumble that Clarissa felt she'd better ignore.

They took plates and selected some food. Since Edouard seemed to have difficulty in making small talk, Clarissa gave him a light-hearted description of her first ten days in Switzerland. She was rewarded when he began to laugh as she told him how she had been saved the expense of an alarm clock since she was shaken awake each morning by the machinery on the building site next door.

'Good gracious! Does it go on like that all the time?'

'A lasting noise, as horrid and as loud
As Thunder makes, before it breaks the cloud'

'That's from an English poem by—'

'Yes, I know, by Edmund Waller. A very much neglected poet. You English have so many that you can afford to neglect some.'

'You know English poetry?' she asked, greatly impressed.

'I read it at university, did a thesis on lesser names of the seventeenth century. Do you know that song of Waller's:

Go, lovely rose!
Tell her; that wastes her time and me—'

'Oh yes! It's beautifully set to music.' She sang the next line or two softly, so that he leaned closer to her.

He produced a rueful smile. 'I'm sure it's delightful, but sad to say I'm completely tone-deaf. I only know when the National Anthem is being played because everyone stands up.'

She gave a peal of laughter. 'But that's gorgheous! If friends ganged up to play a joke on you they could get you to stand to attention for the Charleston!'

'I'm afraid,' he said, the ruefulness increasing, 'I

don't have enough friends to make that possible.'

'Oh, surely! Friends from your university days—?'

'All drifted away. You see, they shared my interests then, but now that I'm trapped in this dull office job—'

'Do you work for Monsieur Pagel?'

'For Roland? God forbid! The pace he keeps going would kill me! No, Papa wanted me to follow him into the Corps Diplomatique, but I didn't seem to get the right chances and so instead I've ended up in what he considers a "home for failed diplomats"—the Bureau of the United Nations Organisation.'

'But that must be fascinating!' she exclaimed. 'I've walked along the lake shore and seen the grounds—I've often thought it would be marvellous to go inside and find out what goes on.'

'Really? Would you like to? It would be a great pleasure to show you round, *mademoiselle*.'

'I should love to come.' She looked at him expectantly.

'Well . . . next week? May I ring you?'

'That would be lovely. Give me a piece of paper and I'll write down my number.'

They had to find a place to set down plates and glasses. Then he produced, not a piece of paper, but a neat little morocco-bound address book. She wrote in capitals: Clarissa Oakley, then her address and telephone.

'Clarissa,' he read. 'A beautiful name. There's a very famous and sad novel about a girl called Clarissa—'

'Yes, by an eighteenth-century writer whom nobody reads any more.'

'I shall make a point of reading it . . . Clarissa.'

'Shall you . . . Edouard?'

They were smiling companionably at each other as a third voice joined the conversation.

'First-name terms after five minutes' acquaintance! Fast work, Miss Oakley.'

She turned with a mixture of surprise and appre-hension. 'I hope you don't disapprove, Monsieur Pagel?'

Her employer raised expressive eyebrows. 'At a time of national high jinks, we should all seize our chances . . . *Clarissa*.'

'It certainly leads to a less formal atmosphere . . .

Roland.'

She held her breath after she had said it, expecting to see from his expression that she had gone too far. But to her astonishment he laughed aloud.

He was about to make some remark when he was checked by an irritable voice saying: 'Really, *mademoiselle*, you seem to have a most remarkable talent for promoting gaiety! First my brother and now Monsieur Pagel.'

Roland Pagel moved aside to allow the speaker to join them. And Clarissa found herself meeting the cool assessment of Simone Masagram's unfriendly brown eyes.

CHAPTER III

Afterwards, it struck Clarissa that from this moment the upper échelon guests seemed to move from the corner of the room which they had occupied, and to clump round Edouard and herself. Of course they came because Roland Pagel had come. What wasn't so clear, then or afterwards, was why Roland had bestirred himself from among his friends.

He said it was because he wanted to know what she and Edouard were talking about. But why should that interest him? This was exactly the point that Simone Masagram took up.

'It's a change to find anyone bothering to find out what Edouard is talking about,' she observed, with a momentary smile that didn't quite take the sting from her words.

'Th-that's exactly what I was th-thinking,' Edouard replied. He darted a glance at his sister. 'Perhaps Roland really wanted to find out what Clarissa was saying.'

'That's possible, I suppose,' she agreed airily. 'Perhaps Clarissa has a talent for tantalising as well as amusing?'

'Neither, *mademoiselle*,' Clarissa assured her. 'It just happens that your brother and I struck up a con-

49

versation about poetry—'

'About *what?*'

'English poetry. We were discussing Edmund Waller.'

'A likely story!' chirruped a wit from the edge of the group.

'It's qu-quite true,' Edouard said with some anxiety. 'We—'

'Of course, my brother read English at university,' Simone recalled. She cast a glance of bright malice at her host. 'There Roland, *mon cher*—that puts you under a decided handicap. I don't suppose you know the names of two poets, either French or English.'

'Very true,' agreed Roland. 'I know all about stressed concrete and girder construction, but as you seem to be well aware, Simone, I'm a cultural ignoramus.'

'Oh!' She pursed her lips. 'I didn't exactly mean *that*—'

Edouard intervened, looking even more anxious. 'Some people have a natural bent towards poetry. It's n-nothing to do with culture—'

'Come, come, that's nonsense,' his father cut in. 'As usual, Edouard, you overstate the case. What I think you meant is that many men of culture are not the least interested in poetry, which is not the same thing as saying poetry has nothing to do with culture.'

'Now that we've put Edouard in his place,' Roland said with dryness, 'may I come back to what I asked in the first place? What was it about this English poet that you and Edouard found so amusing, Clarissa?'

'I forget. Whatever it was, it hardly seems worth all this post-mortem,' she returned, her tone as dry as his. The attitude of both Simone and Simone's father towards Edouard had distressed her; no wonder he seemed so unsure of himself if his family continually treated him as if he were some sort of village idiot. 'Edouard was telling me that you are in the Diplomatic Corps, Monsieur Masagram?'

The older man frowned. 'I *was*,' he said. 'Unfortunately my career was cut short by ill-health—some mysterious germ I picked up in a posting to a tropical land.'

'I'm so sorry.'

'Such things happen in the service of one's country. My chief regret is that my family name no longer appears in the ranks of those who carry out ambassadorial duties—'

'Did you ever serve in London?' Clarissa broke in, seeing Edouard colour painfully at his father's remarks.

'Yes indeed. A most interesting post, my London tour. As Edouard perhaps told you, he was a brilliant English scholar, so it seemed natural to expect that one day he too would serve in the London Embassy—not, of course, in any very high position at first, but it did seem possible he might make his way in some cultural role—'

'Excuse me, Clarissa,' Edouard mumbled, 'I've just seen a friend of mine across the room.'

He made his escape. It caused a break in his father's monologue, so that conversation became more general. Roland said to Clarissa: 'You told me you liked parties. Are you enjoying this one?'

'Very much.'

'No criticisms? No complaints to make to Monsieur Pagel?'

'We-ell . . .' she murmured, reacting to the teasing tone.

'Something wrong? Please tell me what, so that I can remedy it.'

'I rather expected some folk-music, and a few national costumes. After all, this *is* the eve of Liberation Day.'

'You have my apologies. Next year I shall make sure to invite some of my friends from the mountains to arrive in their *bredzons* and aprons.'

'But who knows whether I shall be here next year?'

He said sharply: 'You are planning to be elsewhere?'

But before she could reply his attention was claimed by a department manager. It was Simone who took up the thread.

'Do you move about a great deal in your job, Clarissa?'

'I'm hoping to do so.'

'Heading anywhere in particular?'

'Upwards,' Clarissa laughed.

'Ah! You're ambitious?'

Clarissa smiled and shrugged, allowing herself to be drawn away by the eager attentions of one of the young executives. She wasn't unhappy to withdraw from the circle; Simone's interest in her was not exactly to her taste, Monsieur Masagram she found rather self-important, and as to Roland Pagel—he still made her uneasy because she couldn't quite understand him.

She edged her way to an unoccupied chair, but just as she reached it a man turned from the buffet with a plate loaded with food, and she found herself face to face with Jean-Louis Blech.

'What on earth are you doing here?' she gasped.

'Having something to eat,' he said, pushing a fork into a mound of pâté.

'But how did you get in?'

'I just walked in. Why not?'

'But . . . but . . . you're not an employee.'

'Neither are half the other people here.' He pointed the prongs of his fork towards Edouard's father. 'Him, for instance. That's Jules Masagram, isn't it? *He* doesn't work for Entreprise Pagel.'

Clarissa subsided on to her chair. 'Oh well,' she said, 'I suppose it doesn't matter. One more can't make any difference in this mob. Have you been here long?'

'Only long enough to work my way towards the fodder. It's superb—can I get you some?'

'No, thanks. I feel if I eat another crumb or drink another drop or exchange another piece of small-talk, I shall scream.'

'My word, that's a strange attitude—particularly from a girl who was right in amongst the gilt-edged securities when I arrived.' Jean-Louis chased a piece of chicken with his fork. 'Didn't I tell you Pagel was taken with you?'

'Oh, please don't start that again, Jean-Louis!'

'I can't understand why you're so unwilling to see it. Look here, Clarissa—this room is full of people, a lot of them very rich or important or both. But who was Pagel talking to when I arrived? You.'

'That was only because—'

52

'Because what?'

She couldn't really find an answer. While she was still hesitating, she became aware that someone had come up behind her chair.

'Good evening,' she heard Roland say. 'We last met in rather different circumstances, *monsieur*.'

Jean-Louis swallowed a mouthful of food with unbecoming haste. 'Good evening, Monsieur Pagel. I . . . er . . . was under a misapprehension at the time. I hope you . . . er . . . don't hold it against me?'

'I never waste time on trivialities,' Roland replied. 'But I am rather interested in how you happen to be here this evening.'

'Oh . . . er . . . Mademoiselle Oakley invited me.'

'She did?' At last he came from behind her chair, so as to turn an unsmiling glance upon her. 'Then of course, if you're Clarissa's guest, you're welcome.'

She saw Jean-Louis' thin face sharpen at this use of her first name. She knew he would take it as further support for his theory of a romantic interest on Roland's part. It seemed Jean-Louis had few scruples about using his acquaintanceship with her as self-help. 'It's kind of you, Monsieur Pagel,' he said, 'and in fact it's a great chance for me, meeting you like this. It just so happens that I've been doing some work for a hotel—'

'Photographic work?'

'Oh, you remembered I was a photographer? I—'

'My friend, you were so hung about with equipment it was impossible to forget.'

'Well, that's very flattering,' Jean-Louis said, either impervious to the irony in the tone or choosing to ignore it. 'I was wondering, *monsieur*, if I might offer my services to you? The new hotels—'

'The new hotels will belong to the Chaval chain. You would have to approach their public relations department.'

'I quite understand that, Monsieur Pagel, but a word from *you* . . . ?'

Clarissa felt ready to die of embarrassment. She quite understood that Jean-Louis needed the work and had to seize the opportunity, but to ask hat-in-hand for favours struck her as bordering on the obsequious. She quite expected Roland to ask why he should bother to say a word on Jean-Louis' behalf, but when he spoke his suggestions were much more helpful—or apparently so.

'There's really no need for words from me when the Director of Public Relations for Chaval is just across the room from you. Why don't you speak to her now?'

'Where?' Jean-Louis asked in eager acceptance, glancing about.

'In the suit of white silk—'

'Oh yes, I see! Thank you, Monsieur Pagel, thank you indeed!' He got rid of his plate and his glass, to bustle his way through the throng.

'I rather thought he was the kind who believed in striking while the iron's hot,' Roland said, following him with his gaze. 'That's the impression he gave from the very first . . .'

Clarissa recalled that at the moment when they had all three come together for the first time, Jean-Louis had seized his chance and asked her out. When Roland turned his head, she saw from his expression that it had been in his mind too.

'When I came over to speak to you,' he went on, 'I had other reasons than giving opportunities to your ambitious friend. Are you serious when you claim an interest in folk-lore? Because, if so, perhaps you'd like to come and see the *feux de joie?*'

Clarissa looked at him questioningly.

'We light bonfires on the peaks,' he explained, 'in memory of the signing of the pact which gave us the Swiss Confederation. It's rather a charming sight—if you go up to a good viewpoint in the Juras you can see the fires coming alight in one place after another. Would you enjoy that?'

'Oh, I'd love it! May I really come?'

'Do you have a coat with you? If not, we'll stop by your apartment so that you can fetch one. The mountain breeze can be cool, and especially in the night hours. Come along.'

He shepherded her towards the door; she obediently went with him, giving her attention to the problem of manœuvring between groups of party-goers. Just beyond the entrance to the cafeteria she found Edouard Masagram waiting with his father, who was puffing rather impatiently on a fine cigar. Jules Masagram took the cigar out of his mouth to say in some surprise: 'You are coming with us?'

'I thought Clarissa might find it interesting,' Roland said.

'Oh—of course. What a pleasure to have your company, *mademoiselle*.'

She could tell he didn't welcome her arrival at all, but said demurely, 'Thank you, Monsieur Masagram.'

'Go and fetch your sister,' ordered Edouard's father. 'What on earth is keeping her?'

'There's plenty of time, Jules,' Roland soothed. 'It won't even be dark for another three hours.'

But Edouard had scurried away. His father roused himself to say one or two words to Clarissa while Roland summoned a doorman to order the cars to the door. After a few moments Edouard reappeared, followed by Simone and—much to Clarissa's surprise—Jean-Louis.

'Come along, my dear,' Monsieur Masagram urged, 'the cars are here.' He hardly spared a glance for Jean-Louis.

'I'm quite ready, Papa.'

'Have you a coat, Simone?' Roland inquired, returning.

'In the car.' She offered her hand to Jean-Louis. 'Well, Monsieur Blech, if you'll send me a portfolio of your work, I'll let you know if we're interested.'

'You're going up into the mountains?' Jean-Louis asked. 'And taking Clarissa?'

Clarissa saw Roland give a little frown. 'Clarissa has agreed to come,' he said.

Jean-Louis cast a reproachful glance at Clarissa. 'I thought we had a date, Clarissa!'

Clarissa was quite taken aback. She knew perfectly well—as did Jean-Louis—that they had no date. 'Why, I—you're mistaken, Jean-Louis—'

'It's a bit sad to be left all on my own for the rest of the evening. . . .'

'Perhaps you'd like to change your mind about coming,' suggested Simone with a little smile to Clarissa.

'Nonsense, Clarissa is fascinated by everything to do with folk-lore. Of course she's coming.'

'But you've spoiled the evening for Monsieur Blech,' Simone insisted, looking from one to the other with malicious amusement.

Edouard, anxious to come to the rescue, plunged in. 'Perhaps Monsieur Blech would like to come too?' he suggested. 'After all, there are four places in the Passat and two in your Lamborghini, Roland—that makes six. Monsieur Blech would just make up the numbers perfectly.'

'Perfectly,' murmured Roland. 'Would you care to come, Monsieur Blech?'

'You're very kind,' Jean-Louis said. 'And since everyone else seems to be on first name terms, please call me Jean-Louis.'

'Such affability is really overwhelming,' Roland replied.

No one with the slightest sensitivity could have missed the sarcasm behind the words. Clarissa stole a glance at Jean-Louis, only to see him blandly following Simone across the big entrance hall. She dared not look at Roland. She realised he had spoken in that way to see just how far Jean-Louis would go to keep his precarious hold on this important business contact.

She too went towards the big glass doors of the Pagel Building. The evening sun was bathing everything in a clear golden light. To her left, beyond the Quai Général Guison, the lake was busy with craft, sailing boats and cabin cruisers decked with pennants. The two cars waited by the kerb, Roland's dark blue Lamborghini and, behind it, one of the latest Volkswagen saloons, a dark red Passat.

Simone, who had led the way, directed Jean-Louis towards the Passat with a little push, after which she herself opened the door of the Lamborghini and took her place in the passenger seat. Roland paused by the door on the other side. Everyone else trooped on to join Jean-Louis by the Passat.

'Are you driving or shall I?' Jules Masagram demanded.

'Just as you like, Papa,' Edouard said.

'Then you'd better let me. The way you hesitate at crossings and road junctions, we'll never keep up with Roland in that racer of his.'

'Very well, Papa. Would you like to sit in the front, Clarissa, so that you can enjoy the—'

'Don't be absurd, Edouard. I need you beside me to look at the map, just in case we get separated from Roland.' He tipped forward the front seat so Clarissa could get in.

'Was he really a diplomat?' Jean-Louis murmured in Clarissa's ear as they settled themselves in the back. 'He seems completely without tact.'

'Listen to who's talking!' Clarissa replied. 'Your behaviour this evening has been incredible. First you gatecrash the party, then you lie about having an invitation from me, next you cadge an introduction from Roland, and now you've elbowed your way into an excursion by yet another lie!'

'All's fair in love and war,' said Jean-Louis. '*A la guerre comme à l'amour!*'

'And which is this?'

'Let's call this unarmed combat,' he suggested. 'Listen, Clarissa, I like you very much—there's something very appealing about you. And I think you like me too . . .?'

'You're taking a lot for granted!'

'Oh, come on, you've got some feeling for me, otherwise you'd have told Roland Pagel you didn't invite me and he could have thrown me out.'

'Perhaps I should have,' she agreed, laughing a little. 'You're quite unscrupulous, Jean-Louis. But somehow it doesn't seem worthwhile to get angry with you about it.'

'You see? I told you you liked me!' He leaned across to kiss her on the cheek, and Clarissa was uncomfortably aware that Edouard could see them in the rear mirror.

They stopped momentarily at Clarissa's apartment so that she could fetch a coat. When she came downstairs again she found that Roland had passed the time to his own satisfaction, looking at the progress on the building site; but everyone else was eager to be away.

Their route took them past the Medical School, along the north bank of the Arve River towards its junction with the Rhône, and then out on to the auto-route towards Nyon. Ahead of the Passat, Clarissa could see the blue Lamborghini eating up the miles. Monsieur Masagram, with much complaining and muttering, followed in its wake.

At Nyon they turned to the north-west among the streets, coming to rest in the market place. Here an open-air fête was in progress; everyone alighted to buy a cup of coffee and listen for a while to the accordion band playing outside a café on the Promenade du Jura.

The time was now eight o'clock. 'I think we should move on,' Roland commented, with a glance at his wristwatch. 'And as you've no coat with you, Simone, perhaps Clarissa ought to take your place in the roadster—'

'But I have a coat,' Simone broke in. 'It's with the picnic things, in the boot of my car.'

'All the same, if Clarissa drove with Roland she'd get a chance to see the scenery,' Edouard said.

'Whatever we're going to do, let's do it,' grumbled Monsieur Masagram, 'or we'll get caught in a line of traffic going up to St Cergue Belvedere.'

'Go on, get in beside Roland,' Jean-Louis urged in Clarissa's ear. But somehow as they reached the cars at the other side of the market place, Simone had quickly found her coat and was once more in the Lamborghini.

The drive up to St Cergue was unforgettable. The road climbed steeply, zigzagging up the southern slope of a mountain green with meadows fringed with the darker shades of pine and spruce; at each curve, a new vista was revealed—sometimes the town below growing more and more toy-like as they ascended, sometimes the French Alps on the far shore of the lake.

'You'd have seen a lot more if you'd been in the roadster,' Jean-Louis said in answer to her exclamations of delight. 'Simone was quite determined to stay with Roland. . . .'

'She was, wasn't she,' Clarissa murmured mischievously. 'Which presents you with quite a problem, Jean-Louis, doesn't it? Should you go on doing your best to throw me in Roland's path, or should you lend a helping hand to Simone, who can perhaps give you an assignment—it's quite a dilemma, isn't it?'

He gave a little annoyed grimace. 'For such a quiet-looking girl you can sometimes make the most startling remarks!'

'Sorry if I've alarmed you. If it's any help to you, I'd really rather not have you acting as Cupid in this imaginary romance with Monsieur Pagel. So that leaves you free to ally yourself with Simone in her desire to capture him. Although, if you want my opinion, capturing Roland Pagel isn't—'

'Here we are!' Jules Masagram announced with satisfaction, swinging the car into a parking area where the Lamborghini had already stopped.

A terrace of rough stone had been built out of the mountainside. The sun was slipping down behind the westward peaks, putting them in dramatic silhouette. The snow on Mont Blanc, so far away, glistened with the sheen of a pink pearl. The high rocks were like some mystic tapestry of beige and grey and black, then as the eye travelled down the blackish-green of conifer gave way to the tender golden-green of meadow and pasture.

Clarissa felt she had never seen anything more lovely. She sought to remember some lines she had read, from one of the old poets she loved:

Who first beholds the Alps—that mighty chain
Of mountains, stretching on from east to west,
So massive yet so shadowy, so ethereal
As to belong rather to heaven than earth—
But instantly receives into his soul
A sense, a feeling that he loses not,
A something that informs him 'tis a moment
Whence he may date henceforward and forever.

That exactly described her emotion. She felt life could never be the same again, now that she had seen how small mankind appeared compared with those eternal rocks. Her own ambitions . . . how foolish, how trivial . . .

'Now,' said Jules briskly, 'let's unload the picnic things at once. There's some lager . . .'

Her mood shattered, Clarissa swung about. Jules and his son were opening the car boot. Jean-Louis had moved unostentatiously towards Simone and Roland, who were picking out and naming landmarks.

'Where are we going to eat?' Jules went on. 'Shall we stay here or—'

'Oh, Papa, we don't want a picnic in a parking lot!'

'No, well, did I say we did, my dear? Where shall we go? Edouard, take the basket. I'll bring the rug.'

Leading and pointing, Jules set off across the road and up a parallel track, carefully signposted in yellow to let the pedestrian know that this was a recommended footpath. Edouard followed, considerably laden with a big picnic basket. Clarissa went with them. The path climbed gently, through a fold in the slope that sheltered a farmhouse where an outdoor party was in full swing at the far side of a terrace of vines.

'Shall we go and join them?' wondered Jules. 'No, perhaps not. Let's go on a little.' Once more he led on. They went through a copse of arolla pine and larch until they crossed, by means of a little wooden bridge, a bright rushing stream. On the other bank the path led on past a clearing and more steeply upward among broken stone and bushes.

'There,' said Jules. 'A perfect spot. Nice and level for putting our plates and cups on, and we can cool the lager in the stream. Edouard, put the food here— no, no, not on the grass, on that boulder. Now then . . .'

Clarissa found his continual chatter very hard to bear. She moved quietly away, following the path upward. The broken stone was sharp under her thin shoes, so she moved on to the turf. Soundlessly she stole away from the busy pair below her as they set out the picnic. Around her on each side there were green slopes clad with bushes and plants scattered with blossoms—she saw mauve clusters of rest-harrow and the tall spears of yellow mullein. Shadows were lengthening now; birds were hurrying about to find the last mouthfuls of food before settling down for the night. She came to more woodland, through which the path rose more steeply. As it twisted and turned she saw the main road curving its way up from St Cergue to the Col de la Givrine. Then, more directly ahead, she saw a slim peaked bell-tower above the trees; the soft tolling of the bell reached her.

She came out on a country road from which steps led down to the grounds of the church. A board told her that this was La Chapelle de Vervange. Villagers in their best clothes nodded and bade her good evening as they passed her on their way to the thanksgiving service. She leaned on a rough stone wall to watch them, to see the light fade on the tiled bell-steeple, to see the lights in the church window glow more strongly in the gathering dusk.

The strokes of the bell ceased. After a moment, faintly, she heard the organ, and then voices drifted in the evening air:

> *La patrie est sur nos monts,*
> *Sur les rocs que nous aimons . . .*

Our homeland is on the mountains and the rocks that we love . . . Clarissa listened, spellbound. It was impossible not to be moved by the words and the fervour with which they were sung. Tears came into her eyes as she stood in the sweet evening air.

But in a moment footsteps on the path warned her that someone was approaching; she blinked fiercely to banish the moisture from her lashes, unwilling to let anyone know of this welling-up of unreasonable emotion.

'So there you are,' Roland said as he reached her side. 'You ought not to wander off in the mountains.'

She kept her head turned away. 'You can hardly call it wandering. I'm only about two hundred yards away from the picnic site.'

'But you were completely out of sight. We were quite worried.'

Privately Clarissa thought it very unlikely that anyone except perhaps Edouard had noted her disappearance; everyone else was too wrapped up in their own affairs.

She made no reply. Roland put his hand on her arm

and turned her towards him. In the fading light he bent his head to study her.

'Are those tears I see sparkling on your lashes?' he said. His voice was unexpectedly gentle.

'Of course not—'

'It's my fault, I suppose,' he went on with a sigh. 'I had a good idea what would happen when I sent Jean-Louis off in pursuit of Simone. But I'd no idea you'd already learned to feel so much for him.'

'I assure you I don't feel anything for Jean-Louis—'

'Good. I'm happy to hear you say so, because even if it isn't completely true, perhaps it will become so.'

'I assure you, Monsieur Pagel—'

'Roland,' he corrected her. 'We're all on first name terms, remember? Jean-Louis himself put it on record.'

He linked her arm in his, and they made their way back. As they came through the copse Clarissa saw the glimmer of something white among the trees, and for a moment was tempted to believe in some ghost of the mountainside. But it was Simone in her white silk suit.

'Roland, you really are the limit!' she chided. 'We were all just about to sit down to eat when you vanished!'

'You needn't have put off starting the meal,' he said negligently.

'But where have you two been?'

'Admiring the view.'

'In the dark?'

'Of course, in the dark. That's why we're here, is it not? To see the fires spring up on the dark rocks.'

Simone turned on her heel and went back the way she'd come. When they all three reached the clearing, it was to find Jules and Jean-Louis contentedly spreading pâté on crusty bread, while Edouard stood looking anxiously towards the sound of their footsteps.

'Sit down, Edouard, sit down,' commanded his father. 'You look so— Ah, there you are, Simone! Come along, sit down and eat, the pâté is really quite good. Amélie's cooking is improving.'

Because it was less trouble to obey, they all did so. When the meal ended it was quite dark. Clarissa got to her feet and walked to the edge of the clearing, but there was no outlook except straight down into the valley.

'Where will the bonfires be?' she asked.

'You won't be able to see them from here. Come, you and I will walk down to the vine terrace—from there we shall see a panorama.'

There was something in the way he said it which made it an invitation exclusive to Clarissa alone, and in a tone rather too low for the others to hear above their cross-talk.

She let him take her arm to guide her in the dark to the bridge across the stream, then to the farm. On the far side of the vine rows, the farm folk had lit lanterns; there was the lilt of music, a guitar and a violin. She could make out figures moving dreamily to its beat.

'This way.' The path was paved now. He walked briskly past the low colonnades of vines. At their approach the owner of the farm rose from his bench to greet them, and Roland replied in the *patois*. He introduced Clarissa briefly, but though she was welcomed she knew it was Roland they were glad to see—a countryman of theirs, a Vaudois, who had come to share the celebration with them.

They were given places of honour on the bench. Glasses of the sharp local wine were offered, slices of rich cherry cake. Clarissa set them by, anxious to drink in with her eyes every detail of the scene before her. There was a half-moon, riding above the massive peaks. Beneath them tree and rock, town and tower, were lustred by the pale light. Far below them shimmered the Lake of Geneva, a pool of silver bordered by spangles of gold that were the lamps of the towns—Nyon, Crans, Coppet, Geneva to the west, Rolle and Ouchy and Vevey to the east.

She couldn't speak: it was too beautiful for praise. Yet there was more beauty to be added. Suddenly, as if by some magic unheard signal, little red sparks sprang up and flickered here and there along the mountain range. For a moment they looked like little fireflies against the dark of the night-shadowed rocks.

Then they grew, the lights turned to steadily-glowing yellow. And on crest and ridge and crag, the flames

63

reached up towards the sky—a hundred gleaming spearheads of commemoration.

For a long time they sat on the benches on the vine terrace, watching as new bonfires were lit. Voices called from peak to peak; the echoes gave the sound back again and again to the solitary *armaillis*, the summer farm-steads high in the Alpine valleys. On the lake below boats passed and repassed, strung with lights, floating islands of colour.

By and by the guitarist thumbed a few chords, then began to play again. The farmer's friends began to dance.

'Would you care to?' Roland asked, holding out his arms.

She went into them wordlessly. Some deep spell seemed to hold her, to impel her towards him. Dream-ily they began to dance to the soft cadences of the guitar.

She was intensely happy without knowing exactly why. It simply seemed that all her life until now had been bringing her towards this enchanted hour among the mountain studded with the yellow gems of the *feux de joie*. Was it the music, or the scent of the mountain flowers on the cool breeze, that had worked the spell? Or was it the warmth and strength of the arms that held her?

By and by the rest of the party came to join them, as did others from neighbouring farms. There was much laughter and singing, many toasts to the homeland and the memory of its heroes. The hours seemed to speed away without any sense of weariness.

But at length the moon began to look paler in the sky.

'It's time to go,' Roland said. 'In an hour or so day will begin to dawn. We'd better go home for some sleep.'

All at once, as if his words had taken away a barrier, sleepiness seemed to rush on them all. They shook hands, clapped each other on the back, promised the farm folk to come back another time. Then they collected up the debris of the picnic from the clearing and trudged down to the cars.

It was very cool now. Roland insisted that the two

girls should ride in the saloon car on the return journey. Clarissa snuggled down in the corner, her English wool coat pulled close against her neck. Quite soon she had dozed off, a happy turn to the corners of her mouth; she didn't rouse again until the traffic on the outskirts of Geneva penetrated her dreams.

'Well, have you enjoyed the evening?' Simone asked her.

'It was wonderful. I'm so grateful to Roland for inviting me.'

'It was kind of him. Surprisingly so, really—he doesn't often bother to put himself out for small fry.'

Clarissa gathered her wits together. She recognised an attack when she heard it.

'I ought to be very flattered, then.'

'Oh, I wouldn't build too much on it if I were you. I know Roland very well—I know when he's just indulging a whim.'

'Roland has never struck me as very whimsical.'

'You know what I mean, *mademoiselle*,' Simone said with a shrug. 'A man as rich as Roland ... He's used to pleasing himself, in everything—even in his friendships.'

'We all try to do that, don't we?'

'But not many of us can be as careless of the feelings of others. All I'm saying, Clarissa, is that you shouldn't be misled. Never forget that you have a formidable rival.'

Clarissa was startled. She would never have expected Simone to make a claim like that openly.

But Simone, having made a big effect, was about to reinforce it.

'Oh, I don't mean myself, my dear,' she confided. 'There's someone whom Roland is quite clearly mad about. People gossip about it all the time, you know. Surely you've heard?'

Clarissa shook her head, although there darted into her mind something she had heard from Jean-Louis, about Roland's reputation.

'He goes to visit her—somewhere along the far end of the lake—towards Montreux, I believe.' Simone paused, laid a cool hand on Clarissa's, and leaned forward to emphasize what she was about to say. 'So you mustn't take any of it too seriously, Clarissa. You do see?'

The car stopped outside her apartment building. Clarissa opened the car door and got out.

'Good night,' said Simone, 'or rather good morning. Sleep well!'

'Good night!' called Edouard and his father.

The Lamborghini had drawn in further up the lane. Jean-Louis turned and waved. Roland had his hand on his door as if he intended to get out.

'Goodnight!' Clarissa called, then hurried indoors.

Suddenly she found she was so tired that she could hardly climb the stairs.

CHAPTER IV

Because she already had an arrangement with Babette to spend the holiday with her, Clarissa found the next day entertaining and agreeable. She was taken for a cruising party on the lake, met a great many friendly people, and once more got home in the small hours.

But that didn't prevent her from arriving punctually at the Pagel Building for the resumption of office routine —quite the contrary, she felt an unreasonable eagerness to be at work again.

'I don't understand you,' Babette said glumly as she watched her take the cover off her typewriter with a brisk movement. 'You look as if you're *pleased* to be back.'

'I'm not displeased,' Clarissa admitted, though she couldn't have explained why.

'Jenny Trevelyan always used to say that in London you got used to an easygoing attitude to work. That's why she couldn't settle. But *you*—you seem to be enjoying it here.'

'Don't sound so accusing,' Clarissa said with a

chuckle. 'Would you prefer it if I wo.:e a long face?'

'I suppose not. Well,' Babette said as if to comfort herself, 'there's one good thing. *Le patron* won't be around to harry us for a day or two.'

Clarissa paused in the act of tidying a pile of papers. 'No? Why not?'

'He's gone somewhere on business.'

'I didn't know . . .'

'Why should you?' the other girl said with a shrug.

Yes, why should she? And what difference did it make, anyway?

The next few days went by quickly; there was still the stockpile of letters, which she cleared, and those that had come in afterwards to which formal replies could typed. When that was done, Madame Gebermann her to work on a translation into English of a brochure the company wished to send to English-speaking customers.

During this time she became much more friendly with the older woman, whose rather forbidding manner was an acquired habit rather than an expression of her real character. Having to act as a barrier between Roland Pagel and the minor irritations of this world, she had assumed a brusqueness that could be alarming. Under this cloak there was a rather nice, well-meaning, and hardworking woman. So quite soon Clarissa felt able to ask where Roland had gone.

'Oh, he's in Milan at the moment. Next stop is Rome, I think. He didn't tell me.'

'But surely you need to be kept informed of his movements?'

'Usually, yes. I can't understand it. He had business appointments for the second of August, but he rang me from Milan telling me to cancel them. I don't know what was so urgent—he certainly hadn't mentioned to me that he was going.'

'Perhaps something came up on Confederation Day? Although I don't see how—the office was closed.'

'That wouldn't matter, *mademoiselle*—so long as he was staying in his Geneva apartment the call would be transferred there by the exchange. When he's at his house in the mountains it's different. He likes peace and quiet there.'

'In the mountains of the Vaud?' Clarissa ventured.

'How did you know that? In fact, yes—he has a house above Vevey, on the slope of Mont Pélerin.'

Clarissa had felt sure his house would be in the canton where he was born, the canton whose badge he had worn for the Confederation party. Somehow she knew what no one else seemed to divine—that he had a strong attachment to his birthplace.

The following Sunday, as she was collecting swimsuit and sunglasses for a visit to the pool at Paquis, the phone rang in her apartment. It was Edouard Masagram.

'Clarissa? How fortunate to find you at home . . . ve t-tried once or twice already.'

'I'm so sorry. I've been out quite a lot with Babette Georgeot, a girl at the office.'

'Please forgive me—I wasn't complaining . . .' The hesitant voice summoned up a mental picture of Edouard, tall, rather ungainly, a constant crease of anxiety between his brows. 'I wondered if you'd care to come and look over the Palais des Nations one day next week?'

She had rather expected that he would forget this offer, and exclaimed in pleasure. 'I'd love to. Which day?'

'I could arrange to take you round myself, in my lunch hour. Any day would suit me.'

'How long would it take?'

'About an hour, I suppose. And then of course I should like to offer you lunch. We have a restaurant on the top floor.'

'Mm,' she said doubtfully, 'I'd have to have an extended lunch hour, I think. Would you let me ask Madame Gebermann? Then I'll ring and let you know —some time tomorrow.'

He gave her his office number, and there ensued some general chit-chat. When she said she was about to go swimming he expressed envy.

'Why don't you come too?' she asked on impulse. 'It's a lovely afternoon.'

'But your friends—?'

'It's only Babette and a few of her *copains*. Do come, Edouard. It's a shame to waste this sunshine.'

He was so shy that it took more persuasion than she would have had to exert on most other people, but in the end he accepted the invitation. The afternoon was spent in a big group with a lot of talk and laughter, ending at one of the *glaciers* that line the Quai du Mont Blanc; Babette, agreeing mournfully that she ought not to eat fattening food, nevertheless ordered the largest concoction of all, a mountain of fruit and ice-cream and meringue and chocolate sauce.

Now that she knew Madame Gebermann somewhat better, Clarissa had no hesitation in asking for an extra hour on her lunchtime; this was granted for the Wednesday. Both Madame Gebermann and Babette were quite anxious to see that Clarissa had plenty of companionship because the girl who was supposed to have shared her flat, Aimée Regenbach, had decided not to come back to Geneva to work—she had only appeared for a few hours to pack up her belongings, say hello and goodbye, and catch the next train back to her home in Zürich. Clarissa wasn't as downcast by this as Babette seemed to expect: she rather liked having the place to herself, particularly as—Entreprise Pagel being the owner—there was no increase in her share of the rent.

Wednesday proved to be clear and hot. The lake shimmered in a heat haze as her taxi skimmed over the bridge and along the quays towards the green of Monrepos and the Botanical Gardens. The gateman at Palais des Nations had her name on a list: her taxi was waved on, and there at the entrance to the building Edouard was waiting.

The moment that Clarissa enjoyed most in her tour was her first sight of the murals in the Council Chamber. Edouard explained that the five giant figures on the ceiling represented the five continents of the world joining hands in an agreement to uphold the rights of humanity. The strange, dark-gold colouring of the murals gave the impression of some old photograph of an event that had actually taken place, or of some view of a mystical event in the future. Edouard smiled in sympathy as she tried to express this feeling.

They had an excellent lunch in the restaurant, whose windows were wide open to the summer air so that one could saunter out afterwards, to sip coffee and admire the view. Afterwards Clarissa spent some time at the kiosks in the main entrance, buying postcards and putting them into the box so that they would be franked with the United Nations postmark. She was writing the last of these when Edouard, who had been at her side, was called to the phone. He came back with the anxious frown more accentuated than ever.

'That was my office, passing on a message to you from Madame Gebermann, Clarissa. You're wanted at once!'

'What for?' she asked, surprised.

'I don't know. That's the whole message—you're to go back at once.'

Clarissa gathered her belongings together while he called a taxi. Fifteen minutes later she was in the lift at the Pagel Building, being whisked up to the penthouse level. Madame Gebermann met her at the lift door.

'Monsieur Pagel wants you,' she said in a subdued voice.

'He's back?'

'Yes, and very annoyed that you weren't here when he wanted you. You're to go straight in.'

Clarissa walked ahead of her into the ante-room, crossed it, rapped smartly on the door of Roland's office and went in without waiting.

Roland was at his desk, hidden behind a copy of the *Financial Times*. He closed the newspaper without putting it down. There was a moment's silence, while he surveyed her.

She had put on a lightweight cotton dress of pale blue and white, and white chunky sandals; this outfit was because she knew that being shown round a building can be very tiring—but it wasn't the kind of thing she normally wore to the office.

'I see you're in holiday mood,' he observed. 'This is, however, a working day.'

'I'm sorry, sir. Madame Gebermann allowed me to

70

extend my lunch hour—'

'To keep an appointment with a young man, so she said. That's a surprisingly romantic decision on her part. I should not have expected her to give you time off to lunch with Jean-Louis.'

'Excuse me, sir, I wasn't lunching with Jean-Louis. Edouard Masagram was showing me round the Palais des Nations.'

He laid by his newspaper, carefully placing a silver paperweight on it as if he feared it might fly away.

'In that case, Madame Gebermann's decision is more comprehensible.' He eased himself back in his leather chair. 'And on the first of August? You were out when I tried to ring you. With Edouard?'

'No, sir, not on that occasion.'

'I see. It was Jean-Louis that time. What a busy social life!'

'I'm sorry, Monsieur Pagel. I'd no idea you'd tried to ring me—'

'Evidently not, since you were out. Well, and did the Palais des Nations appeal to you?'

'It was a little too much to take in all at once—the organisation, I mean. But I was very impressed by the murals by J. M. Sert in the Council Chamber. They're quite different from anything I've seen before.'

'Yes, I've seen them. You're interested in art?'

'We-ell . . . I'm not very keen on dim old paintings by sixteenth-century masters, if you know what I mean. But I like what I've seen of the more modern painters. . .'

'You should take a look at the Jenisch Museum some time. There are some good Courbets there. Do you like Courbet?'

'I don't think I've ever seen any of his work.' Clarissa was quite mystified by this conversation. Madame Gebermann's face when she arrived had led her to expect trouble, but apart from a certain crispness in his manner —not by any means unusual—she couldn't see anything to cause alarm. 'Did you need me for anything special, sir?' she inquired.

'Naturally, otherwise I wouldn't have sent for you.' He pushed the newspaper towards her. 'There's a long article about trends and costs in international construction firms. I want you to translate it for me as quickly as you can and let me have it with four clear copies. I want to send it to Brussels, Strasbourg and Milan by tomorrow if possible.'

'Yes, sir. Was your trip to Milan successful?'

'Successful?' He levelled a strange look at her from his cool grey-green eyes. 'It depends how you gauge success, Clarissa. I certainly did some business, but whether I succeeded in what I really wanted to do, I'm not sure.'

'And what was it you wanted to do?'

'I wanted to rid myself of a malady that was beginning to trouble me.'

She was quite perturbed. 'Let's hope you won't have any more trouble, sir,' she murmured.

He gave a half smile and shook his head. 'Take the paper and get to work,' he ordered.

When she came out of his office Madame Gebermann half rose from her desk. 'Is everything all right?'

'As far as I could see,' Clarissa replied, still quite perplexed. 'He wants me to do a translation—' she brandished the paper. 'Will it be all right if I leave what's left of the correspondence?'

'Of course, my dear. In any case you've brought it almost completely up to date.' The other woman sank back, looking vastly relieved. 'Really, I don't know what to make of him these last few days. Rushing off without explanation, walking in again unannounced, demanding the English secretary before he'd even *glanced* at the urgent messages . . .'

Clarissa could offer nothing by way of explanation. She hurried back to her own office and set to work at once, for it was already mid-afternoon and the translations were wanted by tomorrow.

The article covered almost a complete page of the newspaper and was both wide-ranging in examples and idiomatic in style. When Babette began to pack up to go home, Clarissa was still only halfway through the typing of the fair copy. She shook her head when the other girl asked if she was coming.

72

'I'll stay and finish this. It's wanted by tomorrow.'

'But you could finish it in the morning.'

'No, I'd rather do it now.' She didn't like to explain that she wanted Roland to find it on his desk when he arrived next day. Babette would want to know why she should try so hard to impress him—and Clarissa didn't quite know the answer.

At six-thirty she was on the last page. The building was almost silent; the last few late-working executives were quietly in their offices on the floor below, and nothing broke the quiet hum of the air-conditioning. Until her door opened and Roland came in.

'Still here? I didn't really mean you were to work all night. Some time tomorrow will do for the finished translation.'

'I've nearly done it. I can get the copies run off as soon as I get in tomorrow.'

He crossed the room to come behind her chair and look over her shoulder.

'How much more?'

'Half a page, sir.'

'How long will that take you?'

'Ten minutes.'

'And after that?'

She took her hands from the keyboard. 'I don't quite know what you mean—?'

'What are you doing afterwards? Going out somewhere?'

'Oh ... no ... I'm just going to go home and have a meal.'

'Mm.' He put one finger on her shoulder, lightly. Through her thin cotton dress it was like the touch of a heated steel, burning against her skin. 'Would you like to come for a meal with me?'

'What?' Genuinely surprised, she turned and tilted her head to look up at him. Where he was standing, the evening sun didn't reach him. She couldn't read his features. Had he really said it? Or had she misunderstood?

'I'm asking you out to dinner. A reward for work enthusiastically done. What do you say, Clarissa?'

'Why, I . . . I . . . Thank you, I should love to, but I'm not really suitably dressed. . . .' She flicked at the bodice of the pale blue and white cotton.

'We need not go anywhere very chic. There's a place I know—very *folkloristique*—a wine-cellar which is old and cool and comfortable, and the food is simple.'

'It sounds . . . very interesting.' She had wanted to say something with more warmth, more enthusiasm, but somehow her tongue seemed all tangled up. She thought he looked disappointed, but before she could add anything he had moved swiftly to the door.

'In fifteen minutes, then? We shall meet downstairs.'

It wouldn't have mattered if she'd made typing errors in the last few paragraphs; she certainly wouldn't have stayed to re-type it, knowing that Roland Pagel would be waiting. But as it happened the page was finished perfectly. She set the sheets ready to be photo-copied next morning, then flew to the cloakroom to make ready.

Since coming to Geneva she had achieved a faint tan, which was becoming to her, making her light brown eyes look more luminous. She wore little make-up these days, only brown mascara to accentuate her fine eyelashes. Her soft hair had recently been trimmed and shaped so that it curved in against her neck to lie like brown thistledown, ending in the very slightest of curls in towards her throat. She combed it smooth, put cologne at her temples and the nape of her neck for coolness, took off her blue earclips and then put them back. She was nervous. Did she look all right? Good enough to have dinner with her millionaire boss, even though it was in a simple wine-cellar?

Downstairs, as the lift doors opened and she stepped out, she saw Roland silhouetted against the glass of the entrance. He was standing quite still; she realised that this was typical—he was not a man who fidgeted, who wasted energy. The tall, rather angular figure was outlined blackly against the radiant evening light, the head tilted in a characteristic attitude of attention.

As the doors sighed on sliding apart, he moved—he held out his hand. She stepped forward and took it.

Only after she had done so did it strike her as strange that he had not offered his arm.

Together they went out into the warm evening. As they did so Clarissa was aware that the hall porter was staring after them with unconcealed interest.

That was when it rushed in upon her, the flood of recollection she had kept dammed up until now. Jean-Louis had said it: 'He's taken a fancy to you.' It was a thing that happened—had happened before. So naturally the hall porter was intrigued. She had little doubt that by next morning the news would have spread: Monsieur Pagel had been seen hand-in-hand with the little English secretary.

Outside she expected to see the Lamborghini, but no— he drew her on along the pavement. 'Let's walk,' he said. 'The restaurant is up the hill near the old fortifications—not far.'

They strolled up the Rue de la Tour Maîtresse, and then through lanes and alleys whose names she didn't know. To Clarissa there was a dream-like quality about that walk; she could scarcely believe that it was happening, yet his fingers were cool and firm around hers, his arm was ready to support her as they went up a steep, cobbled slope.

The restaurant was truly as he had described: a wine-cellar in the basement of a wine-merchant's premises, down four stone steps. The walls were rough plaster, the ceiling was supported by blackened beams, the tables were wine-barrels covered with rough linen cloths. When the waiter came to offer them the menu, he was clad in trousers of dark green gaberdine and a short loose waistcoat edged with yellow cord.

The names of the dishes meant nothing to Clarissa, since they were in Romansch, so she asked Roland to choose for her. When he had ordered he summoned a gnome-like old man and gave him a handful of coins. Seeing Clarissa look puzzled, he explained: 'They have a very old music-machine here—it's a sort of glorified musical box. You feed it with coins and it plays tunes from the nineteen-hundreds—I thought it would amuse you.'

Sure enough, a moment later she heard a sweet tinkling melody drifting through the air. She smiled. 'That's charming. Do you know the tune?'

'It's a herding song from the Jura—"*Veni tote à la montagne.*" '

'I'm always astounded at the way everyone speaks half a dozen languages here—you all seem to be fluent in French, German and Italian, and often in English too. And then there are these dialects that sound a bit like French or a bit like German.'

'You know what they say about us? We can express ourselves in half a dozen ways yet never say what we really mean.'

'Who says that?' she inquired mischievously. 'Envious neighbours?'

'Perhaps. But they could be right. I don't believe we're very articulate people—we're not particularly clever with words.'

'Oh, I wouldn't say that,' she demurred, thinking of Jean-Louis. 'And in any case—'

'What?'

'Some things don't really need words. The important things.'

He studied her in the soft light of the shaded candle. 'That strikes me as a typically English attitude.'

'Really? In what way?'

'It's romantic, poetic, impractical.'

'Is that the impression I give?' she asked, with a little laugh. 'I assure you it's quite inaccurate. I'm a very practical person.'

'You are?'

'I hope so! I trained long and hard to get where I am today.'

'Oh, I see. You're talking of your business self. Is that your real self?'

'But of course,' she said with conviction.

'So when you befriend Edouard Masagram—is that the practical side of your nature?'

'Well . . . I don't really think one can tabulate friendships like that. Edouard seemed to me to need—' She cut herself short. She had been about to say something that would sound like a criticism of Simone Masagram, who was Roland's friend.

'And what about Jean-Louis Blech? In his case, is there some need that you're assuaging?'

'No, that's different. In many ways Jean-Louis is quite the opposite of Edouard. It's strange—that hadn't occurred to me before.'

'Perhaps you're attracted by violent contrasts? Black and white, shyness and boldness—like a coin, with a different emblem on each side. Is that it?' The cool dry voice had a teasing note.

'You may be right. I do remember that when I was a little girl I only liked fairy stories that either had a very wicked witch or a very noble knight. It's all part of the pattern, I suppose. How dreadful! If my mother had insisted on reading Puss-in-Boots to me, my life might have been quite different.'

'And would you prefer that?'

'Oh no,' she said at once. 'I like it as it is now.'

He smiled. 'I'm glad.'

A girl with a basket was moving from table to table in the restaurant. Roland lifted his hand, and she threaded her way to his side, holding out the basket for his inspection. On the shallow wicker tray lay little nosegays of field flowers—marguerites, purple clovers, marigolds. Roland studied them for a moment, then selected a tightly-bound cluster of cornflowers.

'These match your dress,' he said, and held them out to Clarissa.

The flower-girl supplied a pin. Clarissa, with fingers that trembled unaccountably, pinned them to the neckline of her dress.

Almost at once the waiter came with the first course. Because she was strangely moved by the gift of these simple flowers, Clarissa blundered into speech.

'Do you like your life as it is now, Roland?'

'At this moment? Yes, I think I might say I'm pleased with my situation. For a while I was—shall we say—unsettled. But now I've made up my mind and life looks good to me.'

She wondered if it was business problems he meant—

the problems that had called him away so unexpectedly to Milan and Rome. Or was it something more personal? Something to do with being here with her?

She caught herself up as the thought came to her. She mustn't allow such idiocies to occupy her mind. What if Jean-Louis put forward his hints and prophecies—! It was all wishful thinking on his part, hoping that through Clarissa he could work up some sort of friendship with a millionaire. Simone Masagram had put all that in its proper perspective when they came back in the early morning light from the night in the Juras. 'There's someone whom Roland is quite clearly mad about . . . so you mustn't take any of it too seriously, Clarissa.'

'What are you thinking?' Roland demanded, breaking in on the recollection.

'About . . . about something Simone said.'

'What did she say?'

'Just . . . general good advice.'

'About what? Simone's advice has a sliding scale of value. About business, for instance, she's completely dependable. When you said you yourself were a practical person, it occurred to me that Simone had described you in that way. She said you were practical—and ambitious.'

Clarissa nodded. 'That's quite true. I want to make something of my life.'

'If I remember rightly, Simone said you'd told her you wanted to move up among the important people.'

'I believe I did say something like that to her . . .'

Somehow it seemed a cold, hard ambition. She averted her gaze, looking towards the corner of the room from which the sweet tinkling music was coming. Yet she could feel his eyes upon her.

'If it's what you want, Clarissa, I can arrange it very easily.'

'Why should you bother?' she asked, her lips shaping the words with unexpected difficulty.

'Why not? It might be amusing.'

'Oh. Well . . . thank you very much.'

She couldn't have explained why, but from that moment the rapport between them seemed to diminish. Once she had mentioned Simone, a more brittle note came into their talk. She couldn't tell afterwards whether it had been her fault or his, or anybody's fault. Perhaps she had read more into the gift of the nosegay than had ever been intended; perhaps it had only been the casually goodnatured impulse of a man passing an idle evening with an employee to whom he owed a small debt of gratitude. 'Good labour relationships,' as the newspaper jargon would have reported.

When the meal was over, he called a taxi, handed her into it, gave her address to the driver, and said a polite: 'Goodnight. Sleep well!' as she was driven away. So much for Jean-Louis and his notions about a dawning romance: nothing could have been more formal than that farewell!

The extraordinary thing was, she couldn't decide whether she was relieved or disappointed.

About halfway through the afternoon of the next day Babette said to her with studied casualness: 'What did you do last night? Anything interesting?'

It was quite clear to Clarissa that during her lunch-hour Babette had been tuned in to the office radar system.

'I worked late,' Clarissa replied, 'on that translation. And then Monsieur Pagel took me out for a meal, as his way of saying thank you.'

'Oh, really?'

'Yes, really. At ten o'clock he put me in a taxi outside the restaurant and waved me goodbye.'

'*Très bien*,' said Babette. 'That's quite a good way to spend the evening, holding hands with Roland Pagel.' Her eyes were sparkling with animated attention.

'Don't be silly. We didn't hold hands.'

'What is it about you?' Babette went on, studying her. 'Two years now *I* have been in this office, and have worked late from time to time, but never have I been taken to dinner.'

'Now, Babette, be serious—'

'Ah yes—serious. Clarissa, may I just say one

79

serious word? I don't know what you feel about office romances—I don't know what you feel about *this* one—'

'Babette, will you listen to me? There *is* no romance—'

'Not yet, perhaps. It may be that you're the sort of girl who can keep clear of involvements. But just in case you are not, I feel I ought to warn you. Don't take anything too seriously. In the first place, the formidable Mademoiselle Masagram stands in your way. And in the second place, it's common gossip that Monsieur Pagel has a woman friend who means a great deal to him.'

Clarissa frowned. 'I don't think we should discuss Monsieur Pagel, Babette.'

'We're not discussing him, we're discussing you. I just don't want you to be under any misapprehension.'

'Thank you. I know you mean well. But as a matter of fact I'd already had a warning of this kind—and just as unnecessary!'

'From whom? Oh, from La Masagram, I bet! Yes, if ever Roland Pagel feels like transferring his devotion, La Masagram wants to be the new beloved. And if it was a thing that could be achieved by working hard at it, she certainly deserves to succeed. I sometimes think she may actually bring it off, through sheer persistence.'

Despite herself, Clarissa was forced to laugh at the other girl's airy estimate of the efforts of the handsome and successful Simone. 'How can you, Babette! You talk as if it's some sort of business deal she's working on.'

'No, it's more than that. He means a lot to her, our *patron*.' Babette suddenly shot a sharp glance at Clarissa. 'What do *you* think of him?'

'What? Oh ... he's ... clever, and ... and dynamic ...'

'And instead of firing you on the spot yesterday because you weren't here when he wanted you, he took you out to dinner.'

'I explained that.'

'You think you explained it. To me it's still a puzzle. When you were dragged back from your lunch, what did Monsieur Pagel say to you?'

'He asked me if I'd enjoyed my tour of the Palais des

Nations, and when I said I liked the murals we talked about art for a while. He said I should go to the Jenisch Museum. Where is it, by the way? I can't seem to find it in the phone book.'

'Not in Geneva. It's in Vevey.'

'Oh, I see. I'll have to leave it until some weekend, then. I'd rather thought of dropping in one lunchtime, but Vevey's quite a long way off.'

'Half an hour or so on the train. But you're surely not going to bother to go to a museum just because Monsieur Pagel recommended it?' And seeing Clarissa go pink and look confused, Babette pursed her lips. 'Are you *sure* there's no romance?' she inquired.

Whatever the relationship between Clarissa and her employer, it moved a stage further on the following day. She had been called to his office to receive instructions and to take dictation. When he laid aside the last document he stayed for a moment in thought. Then he said, 'Tomorrow's Saturday. I'm having some people to a poolside party at my house at Mont Pélerin. I should like you to come if you are free.'

Clarissa was so surprised that for a moment she could not find a word to say. 'A party?' she echoed.

'Are you free?'

'Why, yes. It's very kind—'

'Not entirely. Madame Gebermann tells me that while I was away you made a beginning on the brochure about Entreprise Pagel as an international organisation?'

'Yes, sir, I've done two pages so far.'

'I should like to see what you've done, and talk over how to extend it with some new material. It's quite important—I'm going to a conference in New York next month and I should like to take the English version with me, even if only as a typescript. Do you think you can finish it in three weeks?'

'I could certainly try. If you'll let me know exactly how you want it—?'

'It seems to me that if you were to stay at Le Blason for two weeks or so, and concentrate on the brochure—'

'At Le Blason, sir?'

'That's the name of my house. It means coat of arms,

81

which may be why I bought it—because, being of rather humble origins, I have no coat of arms of my own.'

Clarissa's mind was whirling with all the things that had been said or hinted in the last few weeks. Uncertainty was reflected in her amber-coloured eyes. Stay at his house in the mountains . . .?

'I hadn't realised you were suggesting I should stay,' she began in an undisciplined rush of words.

'It seems a sensible idea. I hear, moreover, that the girl with whom you were supposed to share in Geneva has left you in the lurch. It must be rather lonely for you.'

'But I don't find it lonely—'

'Nevertheless I don't approve. When employees have to move to a new city, I like to think that Entreprise Pagel looks after them. So while the Personnel Department finds you a suitable companion to replace the other girl, I want you to stay at Le Blason.'

'Monsieur Pagel, I really don't think—'

'What don't you think?'

'That it's any improvement in my situation to move me into your own home.'

'Comment?' He raised his straight eyebrows. 'Ah, I understand. You're considering your good name. Well, Clarissa, set your mind at rest. You will be quartered in the house by the lake where my gardener and his wife and four-year-old son are installed. Does that meet your objections?'

Mutely she nodded. How could she have been so silly as to let her imagination run away with her!

'That is arranged, then. If you can be ready by ten o'clock tomorrow morning, I will send a car for you. And remember, tomorrow is an outdoor party—if you care to swim, there is a pool; there may be tennis if enough people wish to play. In the evening I shall be taking my guests out to a nightclub, so you had better bring an evening dress. Is there anything else I should tell you?'

'Do I need to bring my portable typewriter—'

'Good heavens, of course not! You will find all the equipment you need. Do you imagine this is the first time I have worked with a secretary at Le Blason?'

'I'm sorry, sir—that was silly of me.'

'Yes,' he said in a cold voice, 'it was. Try to be a little more adult about this plan—all I am doing is moving your place of work from an office block in Geneva to a country house above Vevey. Is that understood?'

'Yes, Monsieur Pagel.'

'Very well. You may go.'

She went. When she reached the office she shared with Babette she found her colleague waiting for her with anxiety which was tinged, all the same, with excitement.

'What happened? You've been gone an awfully long time.'

Since it couldn't possibly remain a secret, Clarissa told her. Babette's blue eyes grew round in astonishment. '*Ma foi!* To stay at Le Blason?'

'Yes, so as to concentrate on the English brochure.' Clarissa glanced at her friend and then away. 'He said . . . he worked from there before . . .?'

'Oh yes. During the winter he sometimes stays there a week or two. There's good skiing up there. And then in the spring of this year—I think it was April: he spent ten days or so planning the construction schedules for the new Chaval hotels in Geneva and Milan. Sheets of figures came down by special messenger every day. I can tell you, it isn't a rest cure! Madame Gebermann needed two days off to recover afterwards.'

'Oh,' Clarissa said, much relieved, 'Madame Gebermann has stayed at Le Blason?'

'Ye-es. But Madame Gebermann is a middle-aged widow, Clarissa. And *she* has never been invited to a Saturday party.'

But Clarissa had been reassured by what Babette had told her about the work situation. 'The party invitation is just to say thank you in advance,' she suggested, adding with a little laugh, 'In place of getting two days off afterwards to recover.'

'Mm . . .' Babette looked unconvinced. After a moment she said: 'Clarissa, it could be a dangerous situation. Monsieur Pagel is probably concerned with getting on with a tricky piece of work, but you *will* be in a much closer relationship with him up at Le Blason than you are here. And—say what you like—you're by no means indifferent to him.'

'Don't talk nonsense, Babette! It's strictly a business relationship.'

'Then why are you blushing?'

'Because you're embarrassing me, that's all!'

There was evidence it was a 'strictly business relationship' next morning when the car came to collect her. It was not Roland in the dark blue Lamborghini but a uniformed chauffeur in a grey Rolls-Royce. He handed her in, stowed her case in the boot, and whisked her off to the accompaniment of admiring stares from the *concièrge*. Although there was a great deal of tourist traffic coming in and going out of Geneva, in no time at all they were climbing the *corniche* route into the mountains. From time to time there was a glimpse of Geneva and the plume of water from its famous lake fountain, but then they turned off the auto-route, up steeper, more winding mountain roads into a high valley. At length they turned in between tall gateposts of carved white stone showing heraldic beasts from the Swiss cantons: the chamois of the Grisons, the lions of Thurgan, the mountain ram of Schaffhausen.

The driveway was lined with birch trees, whose silvery slender trunks gleamed in the strong sunlight. Between them Clarissa could see lawns and flowering shrubs. In the distance water gleamed—the little lake belonging to the estate, and beside it a white house, stone-built but in the chalet style and not very big: presumably the gardener's home. Then the drive took a turn to the left. Cars were parked along it, seven or eight of them; and at the next turn in the lane the big house came into view.

It was of grey stone, and clearly very old. Here and there patches of yellow lichen had attached themselves in the crevices, while from every window-sill pink and white geraniums cascaded in a flourish of colour and green leaf. Over the square, sturdy doorway a vine was growing, its green grapes already well formed.

On the paved courtyard the Rolls drew up. A woman

in a dark green dress and white apron opened the massive oak door. She murmured a greeting, took Clarissa's case, and led her through the house and down a rose-bordered path to the chalet. The place was bigger than Clarissa had expected; once inside the housekeeper led her up a wide wooden staircase and into a room on the first floor.

It was furnished with dark wood and white embroidered linen, in the peasant style; Clarissa was no expert, but she guessed the furniture to be eighteenth century and very valuable. The floor was polished oak strewn with thick hand-knotted rugs of white and yellow, and the lamps were cleverly adapted from jugs and vases of peasant pottery. The adjoining bathroom, however, was completely of the twentieth century.

The housekeeper showed her the wardrobe and cupboards, requested to be informed of anything lacking, and ended with a message. 'Monsieur Pagel is down by the lake with his guests. He would like you to join him when you are ready.' She led Clarissa to the window and pointed.

The view was over the lake, which—at this point close to the chalet—was bordered with rushes and a little jetty where two rowing boats were moored. But about fifty yards to the right a swimming area had been constructed; the lakeshore had been terraced and paved, a little quay had been built out into the water from which a diving-board stood up. Yellow umbrellas edged with white sheltered white tables from the heat of the sun; cushioned lounging chairs and hammocks were arranged in groups and most of them occupied by sun-worshippers. A few swimmers were in the lake, their laughter echoing across the water.

Clarissa spent some ten minutes changing; she put on her swimsuit and covered it with a button-through dress of pink demin. White sandals, a white velvet ribbon to hold her unruly hair, and white-rimmed sunglasses completed the outfit. She went downstairs and out to the lake.

At first she couldn't see Roland. Then he stood up, from among a group at a table, and came towards her.

'Good morning. Welcome to Le Blason.'

'Thank you, Monsieur Pagel.'

'We will be on first name terms here. Formality is for the office, Clarissa.'

She smiled agreement. He led her to the table, introducing her as 'my secretary Clarissa' before he was called away. She was acknowledging greetings and introductions when a surprised voice cut her short.

'I didn't expect to see you here,' Simone said.

Clarissa turned. The other girl was stunningly attractive in a swimsuit of white and grey silk, over which she wore a loose sleeveless coat of the same material. Her tanned skin glowed against it, her dark hair had a gloss like polished leather. Suddenly Clarissa felt provincial in her dress from a London chain store.

'Roland only invited me yesterday afternoon,' she murmured.

'Indeed? I hope it won't be dull for you—you know scarcely anyone here.'

'There are one or two people here whom I met at the Confederation Day party.'

'Of course. And then,' Simone said, as if struck by a happy thought, 'you know Jean-Louis.'

'He's here?' Clarissa asked. She couldn't really believe that Roland would issue an invitation to him, for clearly he hadn't much liking for him.

'He's coming. Roland told me I could bring a friend, so naturally I invited Jean-Louis.'

Clarissa couldn't see how it followed 'naturally' that Simone would invite him. He had a lot of charm and could be good company, but would he really be Simone's first choice as escort?

A few minutes later, as she was settling down to some serious sunbathing, Clarissa discovered that she had forgotten to bring out her Ambre Solaire. She returned to the chalet in search of it. As she passed through the entrance hall she saw, in the alcove below the broad staircase, the gleam of white silk; but she would have thought no more about it if she had not caught the sharp words Simone was saying into the telephone.

'I know it's short notice, Jean-Louis, but I want you

to drop everything and come at once. . . .'

Clarissa went hastily upstairs and out of earshot. When she came down again a few moments later, Simone was gone, thank goodness. Clarissa shook her head. Why tell silly lies? Why say she had invited Jean-Louis when it was quite untrue? And why rush to the telephone a moment later to invite him? A strange girl, Simone Masagram.

As she was walking back down the path she saw Roland coming towards her.

'So there you are,' he said. 'You've hardly arrived when suddenly you disappear again.'

'I went back for this,' she explained, holding up the suntan lotion.

'Are you desperately eager to sunbathe? Because if not, we could go down to Vevey and just have time to look at those Courbets before the gallery closes at noon. Would you like to?'

She looked at him out of surprised light-brown eyes. 'But your guests—? Won't they wonder where you've gone?'

'Oh, they'll think I've gone indoors to deal with some business. They're used to my eccentricities. Come along.'

He took the suntan lotion from her and set it on a stone urn full of a yellow daisy-like flower. She went with him to the drive, where he put her in the Lamborghini. With the ease of long practice he negotiated the difficult mountain road down to the outskirts of the town, and a few minutes later was drawing up outside the Jenisch Museum in the Rue de la Gare.

Its doors were closed. Even as the car engine died they could hear a clock striking noon.

'Too late!' Roland said tragically. 'But they open again at two.'

'But surely we can't stay in Vevey until two?'

'Why not?'

'Don't you think you ought to be with your guests?'

He gave a little laugh. 'Will it alarm you,' he inquired, 'if I say I'd rather be with you?'

CHAPTER V

That was a happy time. They strolled down to the Grand' Place by the harbour, where the open-air market was in full swing. Beyond the pollarded sycamores the Lake of Geneva shimmered in the heat, blue-grey like chiffon.

'I love the lake,' Clarissa murmured. 'Wherever you go you get glimpses of it, and it always looks beautiful, yet it never looks the same.'

Roland nodded. 'It becomes a part of your life, if you live here. The lake and the mountains ... When I was a boy I used to run down the steep street to the lakeside each morning, to see the sun come up behind the peaks and to watch the swans glide out of the mist.'

'The swans are so elegant. Are they always here?'

'Always. Lac Leman without its swans would be like wine without flavour, or a woman without a smile.'

'That's quite poetic,' she teased. 'I thought you said you didn't know anything about poetry?'

'Very little. My attention has been given to other things.'

'But you're interested in art?'

'What makes you think so?'

'Because you offered to bring me down to Vevey to look at the paintings.'

'That was because I knew *you* were interested in art. I never said that I was.'

'And aren't you?'

'To a very small extent. Architecture appeals to me, because I put up buildings. But on the whole I'm a Philistine.'

'I can't believe that's true.'

'Why not?'

'Well ... I don't know. It's just an impression I have.'

'Then if I'm really very artistic, and devoted to painting and sculpture, why should I deny it?'

'Perhaps because ...'

'What?'

'You'd feel it was a weakness to admit it.'

'Ah!' He gave her a startled glance. 'That's very subtle.'

'Is it correct?'

'I'll leave you to work that out for yourself.' He came to a standstill. They had left the market place and were walking towards the point where the Veveyse River came pouring out of its channel of whitish-grey stone. 'It's too hot to go much farther, and besides, I'm thirsty. Shall we walk up through the woods towards the church? There's a pleasant little café I know of.'

Without waiting for her agreement he led the way by the side of the river. Soon they came to the big department stores at the town's shopping centre, but he ignored this; they crossed the street, took a road to the right, and soon had stepped out of the Saturday traffic of the town into a quiet green world of leaves and flowers.

The way up to the church was steep, and Clarissa's sandals were not ideal for walking. At one point, as she negotiated some uneven stone steps, her left shoe left her foot and tumbled a few yards down the path.

Roland went back after it while she clung to the nearest bush for support. As he knelt to put it on again he said, laughing: 'Never fear, Cendrillon, your prince has found your slipper.'

She was looking down on his bent head, where the strong short hair sprang from his scalp with vigour to glisten in glints of iron-grey in the dappled light. His muscular back in its casual dark blue shirt looked sinewy, powerful. A strange desire to lay her hands upon his shoulders came into her mind.

He looked up. Their eyes met.

He straightened and without a word took her in his arms. His mouth pressed on hers, fiercely and yet with gentleness. In response her hands cradled his head, her fingers caressing the glistening hair. She lost herself in the warmth of his nearness, in the haven of his strength. What she felt, she could not have said—was it delight? Terror? Exaltation?

A moment later footsteps on the path above them made

them move apart. A Swiss family, parents and children off for a Saturday afternoon's shopping, came marching past. Clarissa had the feeling that the grown-ups eyed them with tolerant amusement, and her cheeks flamed with embarrassment.

'We ought to go back,' she said awkwardly.

'Back where?'

'To Le Blason. Surely your friends would expect you to have lunch with them?'

'I suppose there's some truth in that. But I could be persuaded not to bother.'

'I really think we ought to go back, Roland.'

He narrowed his eyes as he studied her. 'Does it frighten you to be kissed? Or displease you?'

'No, but—'

'But what?'

'It's ... taken me by surprise, that's all.'

'And you need time to get accustomed to the idea that I find you attractive.'

'I suppose so,' she agreed in a husky voice.

'Very well. We'll go back. You can spend the next few hours making yourself comfortable with the thought that I'm beginning to want more than a business relationship. So now ... *en avant!*'

He tucked her arm through his and, instead of leading the way on and up the hill, took a path that went along on the slope below the church. They came out on a staircase, down which they went to come out, rather to her surprise, in the street where they had left the car.

When they got back to Le Blason they found an alfresco lunch being served by the lake. Most of the guests were well into the second course, but not Simone: she waved to them from a table on which salad, cold meats, and wine were waiting.

'I've been waiting for you,' she called. 'I knew you'd never be so rude as to abandon us altogether, *mon cher*. Come along—everything's ready.'

Clarissa thought Roland stifled a sigh as he went towards her. 'I see there are four places,' he remarked on reaching the table. 'Is your father joining us?'

'No, no, you know he abhors missing his midday nap.

No, he'll join us this evening.'

'Then who is the fourth place for?'

'Jean-Louis, of course. He's just gone to tell them to bring some more melon—you were rather late and the chill had gone off the portions that were served earlier.'

As she spoke, Jean-Louis came across the terrace and dropped into the fourth chair. 'Hello, Clarissa! Isn't this sunshine gorgeous? Almost as good as the South Seas!'

'The South Seas?' Roland echoed.

'Jean-Louis told me once that he wanted to make enough money to go to the South Seas,' Clarissa explained.

'I see. I hope he soon achieves his wish.' There was a sardonic note in the reply which didn't escape her, and she wondered once again why Simone should have brought to the party a man whom Roland disliked. Surely that was no way to recommend herself to him?

A moment later a servant arrived with their first course, the freshly-chilled melon which Simone had ordered. As they began the meal, Jean-Louis did most of the talking, describing with animation the publicity photographs he was taking for Chaval Hotels.

'The idea is to do a whole series, showing the hotels right through the year and the amenities they offer for a year's residence.'

'A long-term project?' Roland put in.

'Certainly. If you want to show the hotel in spring you have to take a picture in spring—'

'But of course the photographs needn't all be taken by the man who began the series,' Simone observed calmly. 'Although naturally . . .'

'What?' Jean-Louis asked, looking anxious.

'Naturally, if everything was to my liking, I should prefer to keep the work in the same hands.'

'Yes, that would obviously be best. Continuity of observation, that's the point, Simone. No two people see the same thing through a camera lens.'

'So for the sake of artistic continuity it would be best if you were to do all the pictures, Jean-Louis, and moreover, I should like to leave the project with you as a favour to Clarissa. It was through Clarissa that you were recommended to me.'

Jean-Louis nodded and flashed a smile of gleaming gratitude at Clarissa.

Clarissa suddenly saw the whole scheme. Simone, sensing that Roland was beginning to be attracted to her, wanted to put up a 'No Trespassers' sign—she wanted Roland to feel that Clarissa and Jean-Louis had a bond between them which Roland ought not to break.

That was why she had hurried to the telephone to bring Jean-Louis on the scene. That was why she had arranged that they should all lunch together. That was why she was turning the conversation so that it would look as if Clarissa was anxious to further Jean-Louis' career.

To change the subject, Clarissa began to talk about how much she liked the town of Vevey. Jean-Louis disagreed, declaring that the old university town of Lausanne had much more character. Since the other two remained rather silent, it began to be a duet between Clarissa and Jean-Louis—rather as if they would rather speak to each other than anyone else.

Clarissa was vexed by the way events were shaping. As soon as she could she made her escape, saying that she thought she had better unpack. Simone missed this remark, since she was turned away at the time choosing a dessert from the tray that the servant was presenting.

But Jean-Louis jumped up to follow Clarissa as she moved away.

'Unpack?' he repeated. 'You mean you're staying here?'

'For a week or two. There's an urgent piece of work that Roland wants me to do.'

Jean-Louis' narrow face creased into a mischievous smile. 'Ah yes—that makes a good excuse!'

'I assure you it's a fact,' she said with some coldness.

'Clarissa, don't be naïve! He's tremendously drawn to you—anyone can see that!'

She was silent, unable now to deny it since she had had it from Roland's own lips only an hour or two ago.

'So much the better. The opportunities are enormous!

You do realise that Entreprise Pagel use a lot of photographs in their various handbooks and brochures—'

'I know that, Jean-Louis, but I *must* warn you that you've got quite the wrong idea—'

'Don't be silly—if you're going to say you have no influence with him, that's nonsense. He may seem as if he's made of granite, but he'd be inclined to do things to please you, so long as it wasn't bad business to do so. So put in a good word for me, now won't you?'

'Can't you see that, even if you were right, it wouldn't do *you* any good?'

He frowned. 'Why not? I don't see what you—' He paused. 'You mean he thinks of me as a rival? Good heavens, that won't do. I'll tell you what, Clarissa, I'll make it clear to him. I'll have a word, explain that we're just friends.'

'If you do—!' Clarissa was appalled. 'If you do I'll never speak to you again as long as I live!'

'But—but why not? If I'm annoying him—'

'Jean-Louis,' Clarissa said, making herself speak with calmness and deliberation, 'it displeases me very much to have you trying to arrange *my* life so that it will work out to *your* advantage. Even if you were doing it for my sake and not your own, I should still find it distasteful to be handed about like a parcel. I'd like to point out one thing to you. In all your planning, it's never once occurred to you to ask how *I* feel.'

He took his chin in his hand and rubbed his jawline. 'Don't tell me you're going to refuse him?'

'I'm certainly not going to be the next in the long line of lady friends I've heard about.'

'Clarissa,' he groaned. 'You're being absurd. . . .'

She sighed and shrugged and walked away from him, into the house.

When she got to her room she found her unpacking had already been done for her, her dresses neatly ranged on hangers, her shoes on trees, her underwear in the drawers of the tallboy, her cosmetics on the dressing-table.

She sat down by the window, rested her chin on her cupped hands, and stared out at the lake where the sunbathers were now lying in happy silence. At the other end of the little stretch of water some willow trees came down to cast a shade; here she glimpsed a blue-clad figure—could it be Roland?

Her thoughts turned to that moment on the hillside above Vevey, and the kiss that, for the seconds that it lasted, seemed to change her world.

She had felt irresistibly drawn to him just then. If he had been a poor man—or perhaps not poor, but more ordinary, more subject to the laws by which ordinary men live—she might have let herself fall into the deep ocean of love. If he had been the kind of man who wanted a wife and a family and a home, she might have abandoned all her dreams of being a successful career girl, and joined her life with his.

But he was a millionaire, a man of power. Roland Pagel of Entreprise Pagel, used to having what he wanted without any strings attached. Everyone had hinted and warned: there was another woman who had first claim on his heart, and there was Simone Masagram struggling to retain her hold—and who knew how many others?

That was not what Clarissa wanted. She hadn't thought much about love, had ruled it out of her plans to make way for her own ambitions. Yet some instinct told her that if she fell in love it could only be whole-heartedly, and with the expectation of a love as complete and fulfilling in return. No half-way measures; no emotional entanglements that led nowhere except to disillusion; no pretences or deceptions.

She told herself that at this moment she could choose whether or not to let herself fall in love with Roland. And she told herself that it would be better not to. Where could it lead except to heartache? He wasn't serious about her—and indeed why he should want her was a mystery. Perhaps it was simply that she had dared to argue with him: it was a novelty. But when the novelty had worn off—what then?

No, it was better to decide against it now, while she still had the power of choice. If he was angry—well, the worst that could happen was to be dismissed. She could go home, get another job. . . .

A pang went through her at the thought. Go home? But already this was home, this lake of blue and silver with its snow-capped mountains. Well then, she could stay in Geneva, find another post. That might mean that she would see Roland from time to time—how painful that might be. . . .

On the other hand, Roland might shrug off the whole thing. Strange little English girl, turning her back on all that he could offer. . . . What did it matter, after all? To man like that she must seem as unimportant as the paving stones or the blades of grass—easily replaced when she was gone, so why bother to be angry with her?

True, he might be annoyed that even a girl so unimportant should draw back from him; but she sensed somehow that Roland wasn't the kind of man to bear a grudge. He had told her to think about the idea that he found her attractive, but he hadn't suggested she must make any response in his favour.

That was all that was needed—to make no response. She didn't have to say 'no' or make an issue of it; she need only show no enthusiasm for a deeper relationship with him.

A sudden warning light seemed to go on in her mind. Was she capable of that? When he looked at her with that cool, penetrating gaze from his grey-green eyes, asking for her affection—could she steel herself to remain unresponsive?

She would have to try. And, oddly enough, she had allies. Jean-Louis' presence would always be a help. Circumstances had fallen out so that Roland thought she was close to Jean-Louis—had been from the moment they first met. She would let him go on thinking that. It would be a shield, a safeguard.

As for Jean-Louis, he was no problem to handle. As insouciant as a handsome dragonfly, his emotions weren't involved: to him Clarissa was a quiet, apparently persuadable girl who—it so happened—could be useful. She knew important people. He would take care to keep in touch, to be available if ever she needed his presence. He wouldn't expect anything except a superficial comradeship in return, the more so because he was urging her to give her heart to Roland.

Having come to this eminently sensible, businesslike decision, Clarissa rose from her chair, and went to the dressing table to run a comb through her hair. Usually, when she had set herself to solve a problem, she felt a sense of relief. Why was it, then, that as she looked in the mirror now, she glimpsed tears welling against her lower lashes, and her heart felt like a stone in her breast?

She rejoined the others by the swimming area. No one roused enough to speak to her. She went for a swim in the clear grey water, glad to meet the challenge of its coolness, to use up thought and energy on exercise. After a while she climbed out, wrapped herself in her denim dress, and began to towel her hair dry. Jean-Louis dropped on to the chaise-longue next to her.

'Really, Clarissa,' he whispered in annoyance, 'your appearance at the moment is not elegant!'

'It's difficult to look elegant after a swim,' she agreed.

'Did you have to go in the water? How can you expect Roland to admire you when you look like a drowned duckling!'

'Perhaps he isn't looking, Jean-Louis.'

'But he is. In fact he's coming this way. . . .'

Roland, in fact, strolled up a moment later, with a beaker of steaming coffee in his hand. 'I thought you might like this. The temperature of the water up here in the mountains is a bit frosty.'

'I enjoyed it,' said Clarissa, but accepting the beaker.

'I was just scolding her for swimming,' Jean-Louis said.

'Were you?' Roland raised his brows. 'That argues a great extent of familiarity on your part, surely?'

'Oh, no,' Jean-Louis replied, anxious to retrieve the mistake, 'I've no right really—'

'Of course you have,' Clarissa put in at once, in a tone into which she put a good deal of affection.

She thought Roland's face took on a shade of coldness, and felt a shaft of pain—but wasn't it all for the best that he should think she was fond of Jean-Louis?

The sun was very warm. She lay back on the chaise-longue, sipping her coffee. Jean-Louis slipped away, under pretext of taking open-air photographs. Others came to join Clarissa and Roland, bringing coffee from the hotplate. Simone was among them; she said casually that it was so lucky for Jean-Louis to have a friend like Clarissa, who could give him the opportunity to take pictures of a house and grounds like Le Blason.

Roland gave her a quizzical glance. 'No doubt it is lucky for Jean-Louis. However, I haven't given him my permission to take photographs. I'm not saying I would refuse to—but it would have been polite to ask me, don't you think?'

'Oh, I'm sure Clarissa didn't mean to—'

'May Jean-Louis take pictures, Roland?' Clarissa cut in over Simone's reply.

'Certainly. I should like to be informed before he makes any use of them, though.'

'I'll see that he asks you first.' As she said it, she felt Simone's puzzled eyes resting on her. No doubt the other girl was wondering why Clarissa should actively help to build up the picture that Simone wished to present—of a strong bond between Clarissa and Jean-Louis.

It didn't matter one way or the other what Simone thought. The only important point was to create a barrier between herself and Roland, using Jean-Louis as its main prop.

About five o'clock Simone's father appeared, looking rather out of place in casual clothes; somehow his fine grey hair and neatly trimmed beard seemed to need the setting of a dark suit. He seemed in a rather poor humour.

'So hot and uncomfortable in that little car,' he grumbled. 'I do wish you hadn't chosen it, Simone. We were far better off with the Mercedes.'

'I quite agree,' she replied with dryness, 'but it's a much cheaper car to run, Papa.'

'Oh, cheapness . . .' He shrugged. 'That isn't the only criterion.'

'It is so long as you and I have to live more or less on my salary—' She broke off, realising she was disclosing far too much about their family finances.

Her father, unaware, went grumbling on. 'If Edouard would only get a decent job—!'

'Where is Edouard?' Clarissa asked.

'Oh, he's coming, he's coming. He had trouble parking. You know what he's like—if he had a hundred metres in which to settle the car, he'd still manage to get in a panic.' Jules Masagram stared around. 'Any refreshments? I'm as dry as a bone.'

Roland beckoned a servant, and as Edouard joined them cool drinks were served. To Clarissa's eye, Roland looked as if he wasn't particularly enjoying his alfresco party; she wasn't quite sure if it was Jules and his complaining attitude which had brought this about, or whether he had been unenthusiastic before his arrival.

Edouard gave Clarissa a smile of welcome. 'You do look nice,' he said.

She was quite surprised. Her swim had washed off the small amount of make-up she had put on earlier, and the sunshine had put a warm flush on her cheeks which, she felt, would have made her look untidy rather than nice. But she returned Edouard's smile; he was so straightforward, so un-complex, compared with the others around her at the moment.

And, she told herself, that includes *me*. Just at present she was as complicated in her motives and actions as any female Macchiavelli. She had a sudden qualm—was she acting very wrongly? Wouldn't it be better just to walk away from the whole situation, to give up her job and all the hopes she had based on it?

But then Edouard went on. 'I'm so glad you came to Geneva,' he confided. 'Do you know, since I met you, I've had more fun out of life than I ever had before? And the great thing is that we've only just met. There's a lot of fun still ahead of us.'

Poor Edouard! How would he feel if she were to pack and go? She told herself that she would hate to disappoint him by leaving—and that was as good an excuse as any for putting the idea behind her.

It happened that a few minutes later Edouard caught sight of a figure moving about with a camera on the far side of the little lake. 'That looks almost like Jean-Louis

Blech.'

'That is in fact Jean-Louis Blech,' said Roland.

'Really? I didn't know he was coming.'

'He's here on Clarissa's account,' Simone informed her brother, darting a look at Clarissa to see if she would protest.

'Oh?' said Edouard. 'He's your escort, then, Clarissa?'

'I don't really need an escort,' Clarissa explained. 'I'm here to work, not to play.'

'To work?' That was Simone, on a rising note of surprise. 'What does that mean? I haven't seen you do any work so far today!'

'Clarissa's work will begin on Monday,' Roland said.

'She's staying here?' The great dark eyes flashed, and then were hooded. 'It's quite a long way for Jean-Louis to come and see you, isn't it, Clarissa?'

Clarissa replied in a matter-of-fact tone. 'The distance between Lausanne and Vevey is less than between Lausanne and Geneva, actually.'

'Is that so? You would know, naturally. I can imagine how carefully you've measured the mileage.' She turned to Roland with a brittle gaiety. 'You must be prepared to have Jean-Louis dropping in on you quite often, *mon cher*.'

'Any friend of Clarissa's is of course welcome,' said Roland. His manner was crisp. 'But I think it would be only polite to let me know when and for how long I am to enjoy his company. Today, for instance—I had no idea you had invited him, Clarissa.'

'I—' She caught herself up on the verge of denying it. Hadn't she planned to do just this—to hide behind a supposed attachment to Jean-Louis?

'You may grow to like him, Roland,' soothed Simone.

Her father shook his head and wrinkled his nose. 'Can't agree with you, my dear. Jean-Louis doesn't strike me as Roland's type at all.'

'But he's Clarissa's friend. And that being so,' Edouard surprisingly said, 'I don't think we should be sitting here speaking of him critically.'

His father turned an amazed look upon him. 'Heh? What's that?'

'Not everyone in the world is important or from an old family,' Edouard went on with dogged determination, 'but if they are friends of our friends, they have value.'

'What a speech! What's come over you, my son?'

'Well ... I j-just felt ...' His impetus was fading. He fell silent.

The heat of the afternoon had waned. One or two of the guests had gone to play tennis on the courts at the west side of the house. Others, less energetic, were engaged in a game of chess with outsize chessmen of carved stone on a marble board at one side of the terrace. There was a general dispersal. Clarissa found herself with Edouard, sauntering along a tree-bordered path along the lake.

'You m-mustn't mind what my father says,' he began after two or three clearings of the throat. 'He sometimes takes up a very unappreciative attitude, but he really didn't mean anything unkind about Jean-Louis.'

'That's quite all right, Edouard. I'm not really perturbed one way or the other.'

'But Simone says ...'

'What does she say?'

'That you have a *tendresse* for Jean-Louis.'

She made no reply.

'Is it true, Clarissa?' He gave a nod of his head towards the figure of Jean-Louis who, on the opposite bank, was sighting his camera at the massed blossoms of a crimson oleander in a huge marble trough. 'You invited him to come with you today, after all.'

'As a matter of fact, I didn't, Edouard.'

'You didn't? But I thought—'

'It isn't important. He's here, no matter how.'

'And you're glad?'

She had a sudden impulse to be in the clear, at least with Edouard. He was so direct and candid; she could rely on his friendship.

'I'm quite glad,' she admitted. 'I'm happy to see Jean-Louis invited into the company of people he wants to cultivate. I'd like him to have the success he so clearly wants. I'm fond of him, you see, Edouard—in the way one is fond of a naughty younger brother.'

'Oh!' Edouard gave her a look of wonder. 'But he's older than you ...'

'Only in years. In some ways he's got a lot of living to do.'

'I don't quite ... You seem to be saying ... Simone's quite wrong, then?' He uttered this as if it was an unheard-of thing.

'Not entirely. I told you—I like Jean-Louis.' She glanced towards the other bank, but Jean-Louis had disappeared from view.

'Well, so do I,' said Edouard, 'up to a point, but Simone seemed quite sure that you and he ...'

'I don't mind if she thinks romantic thoughts,' she said, searching after a less serious note. 'I'm quite in favour of having a sentimental aura cast over my acquaintanceship with Jean-Louis. Why not?'

'Well ... because in a way it complicates things. What I mean is, I didn't understand what you felt, and so I ... well, I suppose I made a bit of fool of myself, rushing to your rescue a minute ago.'

'Not a bit.' She laid a hand on his arm. 'I thought it was nice of you, Edouard.'

'D-did you? I hated to think you might be hurt by what my father was saying. And Roland, too—he was quite curt.'

'Yes, he was.'

'That upset you?' he asked with unexpected anxiety.

Clarissa shook her head without immediately replying.

Next moment Edouard had taken the hand she had laid on his arm, and was pressing it to his lips. 'Don't be upset, Clarissa,' he said, against the curve of her fingers.

'Good heavens, what have we here?' The voice belonged to Jean-Louis, and next moment he appeared on the path out of the curtain of greenery. 'What *are* you doing, Edouard?'

'Nothing,' Edouard mumbled, letting go Clarissa's hand in embarrassment.

'It had *better* be nothing, my friend!'

'Oh, come now, Jean-Louis,' said Edouard, beginning to recover his composure. 'Don't make such a fuss. You're not going to pretend that you have a prior claim on Clarissa?'

'Me?' Jean-Louis made a big demonstration of it, pointing at himself with a bent forefinger. 'My poor Edouard, it's not *me* you have to reckon with. Whatever gave you that idea?'

Edouard stood staring at him uncertainly.

'Good gracious, no! Your rival's a lot more difficult to compete with. Don't you know that Clarissa is Roland's girl?'

She could see Edouard taking in this question with a gasp of understanding: for him it must all seem to fall into place—her presence here, his sister's opposition.

He gave Clarissa a long, stricken look, then walked away.

CHAPTER VI

In the days that followed, Clarissa was always busy. The work on which she embarked was extremely demanding; it was a thirty-page brochure which now had to be altered and amended and then translated into English. The language was very technical—though she had always tried to keep up with French usage about the construction business, much of it would have been beyond her abilities.

But there was a division of labour. Roland gave her an exact explanation of the meaning, and then it was Clarissa's task to put it into understandable—and if possible, agreeable—English. They worked together very well. Each morning they began at about eight-thirty and broke off for lunch at noon. They resumed at two and continued until six.

Clarissa wasn't sure whether she felt relief or consternation at finding her contact with her employer was no closer than it had been in Geneva. When they were together, they worked. They never spoke of personal matters. True, he called her Clarissa, but somehow in this rather frosty atmosphere she didn't dare respond by calling him by his first name. Rather than use the formal Monsieur Pagel, she generally addressed him as '*Monsieur*'.

She had wondered what would happen at mealtimes. Had she been in the same house it would presumably have been impossible not to sit down at table together—unless he had arranged for her to eat with the housekeeper. But since she was quartered in the chalet, she naturally ate breakfast with the gardener, or rather his wife, since Albert was usually out among his plants the moment it was light enough to see them.

On the first Monday, as lunchtime approached, she wondered what would happen. At about ten minutes before noon she glanced at her watch. Roland, catching the movement, said: 'Madame Luceter will tell us when the meal is ready, but if you are weary we can break now for an *apéritif*.'

'No, thank you, I really—'

'We will stop. I keep forgetting that other people don't find building techniques as enthralling as I do.'

He rose from the desk and led the way from his study. So far all Clarissa had seen of the house was the entrance hall of fine panelled walls and the study, which in direct contrast was fitted in the most modern style with office furniture and draughtsman's equipment.

Now she was shown into a wonderful room with four vast windows opening on to a narrow terrace. The ground sloped away sharply below, but a twisting staircase led down and down between stone-bordered flowerbeds from which cascaded speedwell, bell-flowers, rambling roses, abutilon, lavender, and daisies of many kinds and colours. Since the slope faced east, the care and love that was lavished on the plants must have been enormous.

And the reason why the terrace and the garden were there became clear once her eye travelled onward, because beyond the edge of the grounds were woods and fields, beyond that again a narrow valley hidden from view, and yet further on, the opposite slope—which fell away to the right, giving a view of Lake Geneva. Not the whole of the lake was visible: the stretch of shining water was caught like a brooch against the green of the further shores and then cut off as the mountains came down from east and west to meet and merge in the heat haze.

Clarissa stood wordlessly drinking it in with her eyes. It almost startled her when she felt a glass put into her hand.

'Thank you.' She glanced at the contents, a golden yellow liquid.

'It's lemon juice and peach bitters—don't drink it if you don't like it, but we make it from locally-grown peaches.'

She sipped it to be polite. Since there seemed to be nothing else to talk about, she began on the view.

'I'm glad you like it,' he said. 'Presumably that's why the house was built, for the view—but not for aesthetic appreciation. Two hundred years ago it was probably a good idea to have an outlook over the valleys to Lac Leman. There's been a lot of fighting in these mountains.'

'But I thought the Swiss—'

'Oh, not by us, at least not to the same extent as by the so-called "great nations". But that's all in the past. Now we can look from what was once a nobleman's guardpost, and all we see is a fine stretch of scenery.'

'Have you lived here long?'

'In this house? Only since I became very rich. But in these mountains—yes, all my life.'

'I envy you,' she murmured.

'Because I'm very rich? Or because I live here?' His voice was chill, and she wondered if Jean-Louis' obvious respect for money had led Roland to think she shared his opinions.

But before she could reply, the housekeeper appeared to say that lunch was served.

The table had not been laid in the dining-room, which she saw on a later occasion when Roland gave a formal dinner to eighteen guests. They lunched in the vine arbour, a room specially constructed on the south side of the house with walls and roof of glass so that a very old and valued grape could be cultivated. Despite the fact that the sun was beating down, the room was cool, shaded by the leaves that formed an arch overhead.

Clarissa exclaimed in pleasure, and was prepared to make conversation about the vine indefinitely. But almost as soon as they had sat down Roland's chauffeur appeared with a portfolio of papers.

As he took them from him, Roland cast a glance of perfunctory apology at Clarissa. 'You'll forgive me if I work through the meal. These are papers from the office.'

'I quite understand,' she said.

And that proved to be the pattern for their days together. Each noon, the chauffeur arrived with office documents. Roland worked through them as he ate lunch. First thing in the afternoon he dictated notes to Clarissa or telephoned Madame Gebermann. By three the papers were on their way back to Geneva, and the translation of the brochure was in swing again.

For the evenings, Clarissa was expected to provide her own entertainment; this was no hardship, for Albert and his wife dined very early, after which there was still plenty of evening light for a walk within the estate or up on the mountain paths. Or, if she felt like town occupations, she could go down to Vevey or to nearby Montreux. Montreux, with its summer-resort programme for holidaymakers, was a place where there was always something going on.

Jean-Louis phoned her a couple of times; she was quite sure he did it at the request of Simone Masagram, just to find out the lie of the land. Ostensibly he was ringing to invite her to a party in Lausanne or a visit to the cinema, but she made an excuse each time. When Babette Georgeot sent a message via the chauffeur, however, suggesting they should meet in Montreux on Saturday evening for a meal, she scribbled a note agreeing and appointing a time and place.

The plan went awry, however. On Friday as they were ending the day's work, Roland said: 'You have plans for tomorrow evening, I presume?'

She was taken by surprise. Until now, he had coldly ignored her during after-office hours.

'Well, I . . . I . . .' she stammered.

'You had better ring Jean-Louis and tell him you can't come. I'm having some business associates and their wives to dinner. I need you here to balance the numbers.'

She swallowed nervously. Was she to be the only unmarried woman, and as partner to her employer? How would it look? She began with great hesitation: 'Would it not be better if Mademoiselle Masagram . . .'

'Simone will be here. But there is one more bachelor —or rather he is a widower.' He seemed to relent a little. 'If it is very inconvenient to you, I could perhaps invite the Zuchers to bring one of their daughters. But they are all such dull girls.' There was a sudden twinkle of ironic amusement. 'Surely you'll spare me the torment of making conversation with Mimi Zucher?'

'Very well, since it seems to be a matter of life and death.'

'Thank you.' But then the formality returned. 'You had better ring Jean-Louis at once. You may be able to meet him for lunch instead—the rest of the day is of course your own.' A pause. 'I am sorry to spoil your plans, Clarissa.'

'It's quite all right . . . Roland.'

Perhaps it struck him then that she had avoided using his name all week. He gave her a sharp, long look, then with a nod picked up some papers from his desk and began to read.

Babette was quite agreeable to having lunch next day instead of spending the evening with her. In a way it was a relief to Clarissa; Babette was eager and inquisitive, so to spend less time with her gave less opportunity for questions. They had a light meal on the lakeside patio of the Hotel Joli-Site, which was quite crowded with holidaymakers.

'What a mob!' Babette grumbled. 'Extraordinary to think that in one more week they'll all be gone.'

'Surely not all? While this good weather lasts, they'll stay, won't they?'

'Don't forget most people have to be back at work by the end of August, Clarissa. And parents have got to take their children back because school resumes in September. No, by next weekend there'll be a lot more space on the lakeside all along the Vaud. Might be a few staying on for the music, of course.'

'Oh yes, I saw something about that in the papers. I must get some tickets. Are you going to any of the concerts, Babette?'

'Well, I'd like to, but it's so expensive, what with the train fare from Geneva and back, and the cost of the tickets. Cheapest seat's twelve francs, you know.'

'Perhaps you could get someone to give you a lift?'

'Perhaps. The trouble is most of my boy-friends prefer pop music—they wouldn't walk to the end of the street to hear Mozart.'

'Look, Babette, when we've had lunch let's go and get a programme. We'll see if we can work anything out.'

Getting a programme was no problem. After they had crossed Montreux's busy main street they went into the Hotel Suisse so as to use the lift that would save them the steep walk from the lake level to the Rue de la Gare, and on the reception desk there were piles of leaflets about the *Septembre Musical de Montreux*.

Having studied it, they agreed there was no hope of getting tickets for the opening concert next Saturday, but that if Babette could arrange transport they could book for the following Thursday, a Tchaikovsky programme. This discussion took place on the station platform as they waited for Babette's train to Geneva.

'I say, Clarissa . . . has Edouard Masagram been in touch recently?'

'Not in the past week,' she replied, feeling herself colour as she recalled how they had parted at Roland's alfresco party. 'Why?'

'I ran into him again at the Paquis swimming-pool. He's rather nice, you know. If *he's* coming to any of the concerts, he might give me a lift.'

'So he might.'

'Would you ring him and ask?'

'Couldn't you do that yourself?' said Clarissa, rather reluctant to approach Edouard.

'You're his friend, really. I only got acquainted with him through you.'

'All right, Babette. I'll let you know on Monday if I've had any luck.'

'Is he going to be at this dinner tonight?'

'No, only business associates.'

'Goodness, that means bankers and factory owners. Poor you! You must be awfully keen on Roland to go through all that for him.'

'Babette!' she said, with some sharpness. 'I forbid you to say things like that. I'm dining at Le Blason this evening because my employer asked me to.'

'I wish you'd tell me what's going on between you two,' Babette blurted out. 'It's so frustrating, the way you won't tell.'

'Nothing is going on between us, Babette. And that's the way I intend to keep it.'

Whatever protest Babette intended to make was cut off by the arrival of the big green train. She surged aboard with a mob of home-going tourists loaded with luggage; in the ensuing muddle there was no time for anything but a smile and a wave before the train pulled out.

Clarissa went back down to the main street. She could have boarded the train with Babette and got off at Vevey, but had preferred to take the trolleybus which would set her down at one of the department stores, where she could buy some minor items such as paper tissues and hand cream before treating herself to a cup of coffee. She wanted ten minutes' thought about what to wear that evening.

Bankers and factory owners ... And their wives. She knew they would be elegant women, well dressed in a way that had almost gone out of fashion for the moment in London. Their clothes would be *haute couture*, they would have real pearls and real diamonds, their hair would have had the attention of the best stylist in the town.

Simone would look superb, as she always did. With a sigh Clarissa had to admit that nothing she could ever afford would equal Simone's clothes.

She reviewed her wardrobe's contents. Naturally she had brought only a small selection of dresses with her, and out of the five, only one was an evening dress—the fine dark brown cotton she had worn on her first night in Geneva, and again to the restaurant party with Roland's friends last Saturday.

Although she had had no intention of doing so when she first walked in the doors, Clarissa made her way to the dress department as soon as she had finished her coffee. She kept telling herself it was foolishness: this was a chain store, whose best merchandise would cost not one-tenth of the dresses the other women would wear tonight. Yet she went to the dress-racks and looked at one or two models.

An elderly saleswoman approached. 'Can I help you, *mademoiselle?*'

Clarissa sighed. 'Not really. I don't know why I'm even bothering . . .'

'What kind of dress were you looking for?'

'Oh, I don't know . . .' She had a sudden impulse to confide. 'I'm going to dinner with people who will be wearing rather splendid things and I just wanted all at once to see . . . It was silly, of course.'

'Mademoiselle will find nothing very "splendid" here,' the other woman said in a sympathetic tone. Then, after a pause: 'On the other hand, if everyone else is looking "splendid", perhaps sheer simplicity would make a good effect.'

'Yes, but I see nothing here.'

'It just so happens, *mademoiselle* . . .' Another hesitation. 'What size do you take?'

'Size ten English.'

'Ah! Would you come this way?' She led Clarissa to a stockroom behind a curtain, and from a rail she lifted down a dress in a polythene cover. 'As you realise, *mademoiselle*, the summer season is over and so we were quite vexed when a sample dress came in yesterday which we had asked to see six months ago. We certainly don't intend to order any. But . . . you see . . . it is rather sweet, don't you think?'

It was a long plain dress of handkerchief lawn, pure

white, the hem and neck and little sleeves bound with white velvet ribbon.

'Try it on, *mademoiselle*.'

'But the price?' Though it was starkly simple, the quality of cut and fabric suggested it wouldn't be exactly cheap.

'Well, as to that, I'll ask the buyer. We could probably make you a special price. Do try it, *mademoiselle*. With that pretty tan on your skin, I think you'll like it.'

Once she had put it on Clarissa knew she had to have it even if it meant buying nothing else all year. But the price, when she heard it, was reasonable: she even felt emboldened to spend a little more at a nearby florist, where she had a tiny nosegay of white pinks made up to wear at her throat, pinned to the velvet edging of the neck.

She then took the funicular up to Mont Pélerin, where she telephoned the house and asked to be collected. It was the gardener who came, in a little grey Fiat runabout. 'All the other cars are out collecting guests,' he explained.

'Already?' She was alarmed. She had to bathe and do her hair.

'Oh, plenty of time. They've set off—at least, the Rolls has gone to Geneva for Mademoiselle Masagram, and Monsieur Pagel is out somewhere in his roadster, and I think the little saloon has been sent to fetch lake fish from Ouchy . . .' He chatted on, and Clarissa relaxed. The guests, she knew, had been invited for seven-forty-five and it was still only a little after six.

When at last she finished dressing, she felt she had done the very best she could and that the effect was pleasing. She had carefully set the floppy, thrush-brown hair so that it fell from an undefined point on the crown of her head to the curve of her neck. She had used brown eye-shadow to accentuate the pine-timber brown of her eyes. The dress seemed to skim her figure, defining it gracefully and unemphatically. The little cluster of white-petalled flowers nestled against the hollow of her throat.

She wore no jewellery of any kind. Her shoes were

the plain white leather sandals she wore for lazing out-doors. She had a small white leather purse into which she tucked her comb and a lace-edged handkerchief.

'There,' she told her reflection before she turned to go, 'that's the best I can do.'

It was nearly time for the important guests to arrive —it wouldn't do to be late. She hurried down and out of the chalet, to make her way along the rose-bordered path to the house. The sun was dipping towards the mountaintops; the shadows were lengthening. As she came in by the open door of the vine-arbour, she heard a swiftly-indrawn breath from the leaf-shaded interior. For a moment she could make out no one, then Roland stepped forward.

'I'm sorry—did I startle you?' she apologised.

'You . . . you looked like some little medieval ghost, drifting in from the garden like that.' But his voice was still shaking, though the words were amused.

She must really have startled him. But that was absurd—Roland Pagel wasn't the kind of man to be put off balance by the idea of a ghost.

Quite soon the first of the guests drove up. Clarissa was introduced, and made herself useful seeing that the right drinks were offered. She had quite forgotten Simone was coming until she came unexpectedly face to face with her.

Simone was wearing an ankle-length skirt of wine-coloured silk and on it a three-quarter-length jacket of heavily embroidered metal brocade in scarlet and gold. It looked as if it might have belonged to a rich mandarin of Imperial China. Certainly there wasn't another woman in the room who looked half so resplendent.

Yet when Simone's eyes rested on Clarissa, an extra-ordinary expression came into them—it might almost have been envy.

'Good evening, Clarissa,' she murmured. 'I didn't expect you to be taking part in this affair.'

'Neither did I. It was only arranged yesterday after-noon. Can I fetch you a drink, Simone?'

'I'm sure the housekeeper will see that I'm looked after, thank you.' As if the words were dragged out of her against her will she added: 'You look rather nice.'

'You too. That's a genuine Chinese jacket, isn't it?'

'Reputed to be so. But perhaps it wasn't such a good choice after all. I could perhaps have been a lot more comfortable in a little nothing of a dress like yours.' But then her spirits returned. 'Bridal white, I see,' she remarked. 'A little too optimistic, Clarissa—Jean-Louis isn't the marrying kind.'

Clarissa smiled and shrugged and walked away to direct the servant with the tray of dry white port towards Simone.

When dinner was announced, Clarissa got her first view of the dining-room. Hitherto she had only glimpsed it as she passed the door, but now she was able to drink it all in. The ceiling was high, and from it hung two wide-branching chandeliers of Bohemian crystal holding eighteen tapers each. Under this shimmering, shifting light, the long table sparkled with silver and eighteenth-century German glass. The tablecloth was rose damask, and down its centre ran a garland of dark red roses.

The walls of the room were covered with cream *toile* to act as a background for the paintings. Clarissa felt sure they were Corots, and all genuine; there were eight, two to each wall, perfectly hung and lit by a shaded picture-light. If Roland had chosen these himself, then to say he was interested in art 'to a very small extent' was the understatement of the century.

At dinner her companions on either side were two very distinguished-looking men, one very elderly with a mane of silver hair and the other middle-aged, heavy and balding. He turned out to be from Berne, and perhaps because he spent his office hours handling the funds of a massive insurance company, felt entitled to become sentimental in the evenings.

'Ah, candlelight, the scent of roses, and on my left hand a pretty girl in a white dress! What more could a man want?'

'Good food?' inquired his wife from across the table.

He grinned at her with amiability. 'But you must admit she looks like a little white dove in that quiet pale dress.'

Since Clarissa could see that his wife was not best pleased by his outspoken approval, she volunteered: 'Roland said he thought I looked like a ghost.'

'A ghost? An enchantment, he means.' He rapped on the table with a spoon. 'Roland! Rollé! Hi, Rollé! This sweet little thing here tells me you were not very complimentary about her dress.'

'Oh, now, *m'sieur*, I didn't—'

'It's quite all right,' Roland said from the head of the table. 'I never taken any notice of what Gottfried says except about money.'

'But all the same, Rollé! To tell the girl that she looks like a ghost—'

'I believe I did use the word. If Clarissa feels it sounded disparaging, I apologise.'

Simone spoke up from further down the table. 'She's had a rare tribute. I've never heard you apologise to anyone, Roland.'

He laughed. 'I'm only doing it so Gottfried will leave me in peace to enjoy the fish—'

At that moment the staff appeared with the next course and the conversation was lost. Clarissa had been interested to notice the seating arrangements; she had wondered if Simone would occupy the chair at the hostess end of the table. But no, the elderly Baronne Chénier had that place, with her husband the Baron on her left. So, as far as his friends were concerned, nothing was taken as settled between Simone and Roland—she was there simply as a guest and a business acquaintance, like themselves.

The elderly widower who was Clarissa's 'partner' proved to be a charming man; his white hair did not belie him—he had had a long and interesting life, much of it spent abroad handling the affairs of the company which he now owned. He talked: Clarissa listened. The meal passed without either the stress or the dullness she had anticipated in a gathering where almost everyone was very, very rich and a good deal older. Perhaps because they all liked an early night, they began to take their leave soon after ten-thirty, and by eleven all the guests had gone except Simone.

'Ah, *quel ennui!*' she groaned as she sank into an arm chair in the drawing-room. 'Roland, why do you assemble such a collection of old fogeys?'

'Because I wish to offer them hospitality in return for theirs.'

'Why don't you admit it's for business contacts!'

'That too. I don't see why you should say it so accusingly.' He brought her a brandy glass. 'Why are you in such a bad temper?'

'I? I'm not in a bad temper, not in the least. Although, to be frank, I have something to complain of. You put me between the two most boring men at the table.'

'That was because I felt you had the social experience to handle them. Now, in Clarissa's case, I was more lenient.'

'She seemed to make quite a hit with both of them, particularly Gottfried.' Simone moved restlessly. 'It's very strange—I've never roused that sort of response in him, although I've spent hundreds of francs of the firm's money in trying to be friends with him.'

'Perhaps you ought to buy a simple white dress,' he suggested. 'Gottfried seems to have a weakness for that kind of effect.'

'That's a little too unsuitable,' she said. 'I'm no good at pretended innocence.'

Clarissa roused herself to meet her sharpness. 'Oh, I am,' she declared. 'I'm awfully good at pretended innocence, and pretended good manners, too.'

Roland gave a shout of laughter. 'Well said!' he cried. 'There, Simone—that serves you right! Perhaps I should have warned you—Clarissa may look demure, but under that calm exterior she hides weapons that she can use when she chooses.'

'You've had experience?' Simone inquired, sipping her brandy.

'Oh yes. At our first encounter.'

'You must tell me about it some time.'

'What, and admit that I was silenced by her? Never!'

'Excuse me,' Clarissa said gently, 'but if you wish to discuss me perhaps it would be better if I said good night and went to bed.'

Roland gave her another laughing glance. There was a faint admiration in his grey-green eyes. 'No, no, stay,' he commanded. 'It's early yet.'

'But if you're tired, Clarissa,' Simone said, 'please don't feel you have to stay up just because your employer tells you to. After all, this is a long way out of office hours.'

To her own surprise, Clarissa found herself feeling almost sorry for Simone. She couldn't forget what Babette had said: that Roland meant a lot to her, and not simply as a business contact.

'I think I will go, if you don't mind,' she murmured. 'It's been quite a day.'

'Oh, I was forgetting. You had a luncheon engagement too, did you not, Clarissa?'

'Yes, in Montreux.'

'In Montreux? That's even further from Lausanne than Vevey. I wouldn't have thought you'd drag Jean-Louis—'

'As a matter of fact,' Clarissa said, suddenly weary of subterfuge, 'I lunched with Babette Georgeot.'

'Who? Oh, that little brown-haired girl.' Roland was frowning. 'But—'

'Good night, Simone,' she intervened. 'Goodnight, Roland.'

'One moment—I'll see you safely to your door.'

'Roland—' Simone was clearly about to say that the hundred yards of walkway to the chalet was smoothly paved and lit by lamps concealed among the rose-bushes so that safety was hardly in question. But she thought better of it.

Roland went with Clarissa through the house and out to the path. He drew her arm through his. 'I thought you had a date for lunch with Jean-Louis.'

She made no reply.

'Couldn't he change your evening date?'

'I didn't have an evening date with him,' she said.

'Then why did you say you had?' he demanded.

'If you cast your mind back you'll realise I didn't say so. You simply took it for granted.'

He drew in a sharp breath. 'I did, didn't I? I wonder if I have made other wrong assumptions?'

Once again she remained silent.

'Clarissa, there are things I need to know—'

'No, please!' Her head was swimming with fatigue and she felt incapable of the verbal fencing that might follow if she had to explain her relationship with Jean-Louis. Already she was regretting that she had allowed her guard to drop even to the extent that lunch today had been eaten with a girl-friend. 'Roland, I'm desperately tired. Today seems to have been going on for centuries. Let's say good night now.'

'I'm sorry,' he said at once. 'I know I'm often inconsiderate. Tomorrow, then—what are you doing tomorrow?'

'I thought of going down to the service in St Martin's Church.'

'Very well. Afterwards, we will speak.'

As they came to the open door of the chalet, the gardener's wife appeared; it was clear she was waiting for Clarissa's return before going to bed.

'Goodnight, Clarissa,' Roland said swiftly. His hands gripped hers with a momentary fierceness, then he was gone.

Her heart was thumping in a heavy unbalanced rhythm as she closed the door of her room behind her. She knew by some blind instinct that if Albert's wife had not come on the scene, there would have been some move between herself and Roland—a giving and taking of unspoken promises which might have bound her to this man who already had so much power over her.

Tomorrow . . . they would speak tomorrow. But about what? Did he want to hear her say that Jean-Louis was no rival to him in her regard? If she admitted that, what came next?

She shrank from the thought. If he were to say that they could find happiness together, that she would not go unrewarded, wouldn't find him ungenerous— Oh, if he were to tarnish this strange feeling that had come into her heart, that was growing so strongly although she struggled to uproot it—she could not bear it!

Yet . . . yet his words might be quite different. It was true, he was very rich, very important, very respected. And she—what was she? An insignificant employee with a small talent for learning languages. Not particularly pretty, not particularly clever. Nevertheless, he had told her: 'I find you attractive.' Who was she to deny that there was a strange chemistry between them? And if he found her attractive it might mean that the relationship between them could have more depth than a mere passing liaison.

She told herself not to be silly. Millionaires of the international construction business didn't become serious about little secretaries from the north of England. King Cophetua didn't marry the beggarmaid these days.

But as she fell asleep at long last she heard in the recesses of her heart the echo of the words Roland had spoken as he knelt to replace her sandal: 'Never fear, Cendrillon, your prince has found your slipper.'

She slept late next morning—late by the standards of Le Blason. It was after nine when she opened her eyes to a sky grey with thunder clouds. The fine weather had broken in a building-up of mountain storms, heralded by the grumbling reverberation of thunder in the peaks and occasional flickers of sheet lightning.

'It will clear, *mademoiselle*,' Albert assured her as she sat down to breakfast. 'In the mountains, you know, weather changes very fast—one moment the slopes are awash with rain, the next the sun is drinking up the wetness and everything smells fresh.'

He and his wife had already breakfasted. It had been arranged that they would drive down to Vevey together for the service. Rain squalls made bead curtains across the windscreen as they made a sedate and careful journey down the twisting road, and when the square tower of St Martin came into view, its four pointed grey turrets were silhouetted against a sky of even darker grey.

Yet during the service the sun came out. The clouds didn't entirely clear, but the sky became a patchwork of blue and white and cumulus-grey. Albert and his wife stopped to talk to friends as they came out on the flagstones piebald with drying moisture. Madame Albert said apologetically: 'It's our only chance to see people, at least while Monsieur Pagel is at Le Blason . . . You don't mind waiting a little?'

'Of course not. I'm not in any hurry.'

'The housekeeper told me to say that you are expected at the house for lunch, but that it will be late—Monsieur Pagel isn't likely to be back until about two o'clock.'

'He's gone out?' Clarissa asked idly.

'Oh yes, *mademoiselle*. He usually goes on a Sunday, when he's at Le Blason.'

'Goes where?'

Madame Albert gave a knowing little smile. 'To see the lady in Montreux.'

While the Alberts chatted to their friends, Clarissa stood aside, in a dull and withdrawn silence. After about a quarter of an hour they rejoined her. She roused herself.

'I don't think I'll come back with you just at the moment,' she said.

'But, Mademoiselle Oakley—'

'I can take the funicular up to Mont Pélerin later. Perhaps you'd come and meet me, Albert, or send someone, if I ring?'

'Certainly. And of course it is such beautiful weather now . . .'

'Yes, I'd like a walk.'

A few minutes later she was walking down the steep path through the woods below St Martin's. She came to the very place where she had looked down on those sinewy blue-clad shoulders as Roland stooped to put her sandal on her foot.

She paused by the rail, to stare unseeingly down at the roofs of Vevey. Her eye did not take in the curving red tiles, the golden-brown of the creeper-clad walls, the unlikely line of the cupola on the Russian Orthodox church.

All she saw was Roland's eyes as he looked up at that moment and met her own.

What sort of man is he? she demanded angrily of herself. Last night he had seemed so eager, so sincere.

She could still feel on the edges of her knuckles the blissful pain caused by his fierce grip before he left her.

Yet this morning he had gone to Montreux to visit the woman whom everyone acknowledged as the chief claimant to his heart. Only a few hours after his hands, his voice, had told Clarissa that *she* was the important woman in his life.

But of course there are degrees of importance. Her disillusioned common sense prompted the thought. At that moment he had wanted to make a claim on her, and she, poor fool, had taken it seriously.

A strange, momentary despair seized her and made her go cold. She was no good at this sophisticated game he was playing. With Jean-Louis, at least, one knew where one stood: Jean-Louis was out for what he could get and made no bones about it.

But Roland kept tricking her, misleading her, making her uncertain of herself. She had made herself a promise when first she came to Le Blason that she would not allow herself to fall in love with him, but she had reckoned without the skill he could bring into play. By a deft use of disregard and coolness he let her imagine herself to be safe; and then when a moment's inattention left her open to attack, he tricked her into believing there was some genuine warmth in his feelings for her.

Well, she had her defences up again! Luckily for her she had been given just enough of a warning to bring her to her senses. Now she knew better than to believe anything he might say or imply: she would go back to Le Blason and she would meet him at the lunch table, and they would be employer and employee, nothing more.

When at length she went up to Mont Pélerin she was in a totally different frame of mind from that in which she had begun her day. Gone was the muted optimism, the feeling of anticipation. She rang Le Blason, then sat to await Albert's arrival.

But when a car at last drew up by the Restaurant des Pélerins, she saw to her dismay that the driver was Roland.

He opened the door of the little dark green saloon.

'Hop in. Have you had a pleasant walk?'

'Yes, thank you.'

'The view is always at its best when the sun comes out after rain.'

'Yes, it's very pretty.'

'Very pretty?' He gave her a puzzled glance. 'Can this be Clarissa speaking about Lake Geneva?'

She managed a polite smile. 'Did you have an easy drive to Montreux?'

'Not bad. Quite a lot of traffic, but I didn't get too bogged down.'

'If you'd taken the Lamborghini you could have passed everything on the road,' she remarked, for the sake of conversation.

'I never take the Lamborghini to Montreux. It's too noticeable.'

So he used the little green Renault for reasons of discretion when he visited the lady in Montreux. . . .

After a moment he said: 'Are you feeling unwell? You look rather pale.'

'I'm quite all right, thank you.'

'But something is wrong. You're not the same girl I was speaking to last night.'

She gave a little nod of agreement. 'We all change, don't we? We learn, and gain experience, and with every succeeding day we change a little.'

'And can you change so much in such a short time?' he said in a voice of cool inquiry.

'It isn't really so great a change. It's more like putting things in a proper perspective, realising what's true, and what's important, and what's worthwhile.'

A long silence followed, during which he sent the car competently round the climbing contours of the mountain road.

At length he said: 'Last night I asked myself if I had been making wrong assumptions.'

'I remember you used the phrase.'

'I meant about you and Jean-Louis, Clarissa.'

'Did you?'

'I should like to know if you're in love with him.'

'And I should like to know one good reason why I

120

should discuss it.'

He frowned. 'Is this your English reticence? You prefer not to discuss your emotions?'

'That's a fair statement, I think.'

'I see.' He paused, then said grimly: 'What shall we talk about until we reach the house? Or shall we drive in complete silence?'

'Whichever you prefer.'

'What I can't understand is why you are so icy about it. Could it possibly be, Clarissa . . . that it's some sort of defence against me?'

She swallowed hard before she replied. 'A girl who is in love with another man doesn't need a defence against you.'

'No. You're quite right. How foolish of me.'

And they said not another word until they drew up in front of the house. As she got out of the car he said: 'I left a message about lunch. Did you get it?'

'Yes.'

'You'll forgive me if I change the arrangement. I've just remembered some business I wish to attend to at the Geneva office.'

'I quite understand.'

She went into the house without a backward glance, through to the vine arbour and out to the path leading to the chalet. She could hear the sound of his car as he turned it and drove off again.

After a moment the sound died away.

CHAPTER VII

Next morning when Clarissa came into the house to begin the day's work, Roland's chauffeur was awaiting her.

'Monsieur Pagel wishes you to collect up the paper-work concerned with the translation, and also the two folders on his desk and the file on Montlebas S.A. You are to bring them with you to the office.'

'Bring them? I don't understand—'

'Monsieur feels there is nothing more to be done here —the work is so well advanced now that you can continue at the Pagel Building. I am to take you into Geneva as soon as you are ready.'

'Today?'

'As soon as you are ready, *mademoiselle*. Will it take you long to pack?'

'Ten minutes,' she replied in a voice of iron. 'And five to collect the papers. I shall be ready in fifteen minutes.'

'Oh, no need to rush, *mademoiselle*. The car is still in the garage.'

All the same, not half an hour had passed before they were on the road. The papers Roland had asked for were in a black executive briefcase on the seat beside her; the notes and rough drafts of the translation were in her own portfolio, and her travel bag—with her clothes bundled in haphazard—was in the boot. She was bewildered at this sudden turn of events.

They stopped at her Geneva apartment so that she could leave her belongings. Then they went to the Pagel Building. Uncertain what to do as she stepped out of the lift, she went to Madame Gebermann's office to give her the two folders. When she tried to give her the translation, the secretary waved it away.

'No, no, you are to keep that and work on it as you have time. Monsieur Pagel will look at it when you have a completed version in English.'

'I see.' She waited.

'Yes?' the other woman prompted, already half turned away.

'Are there no other instructions? No message?'

'Are you expecting one?' Madame Gebermann said, genuinely puzzled. 'From whom?'

'From Monsieur . . .?'

'No, my dear, I take it that everything will go on the same as always. There are still plenty of letters in the English correspondence tray waiting to be typed.'

'Of course, I understand. Thank you, Madame Gebermann.'

So this was a demonstration of his anger. She had shown that she did not want the kind of friendship he had in mind, and for this rebuff he was punishing her. She must go back to being one of the cogs in the well-oiled machine that ran Entreprise Pagel.

She was hurt. Somehow she had thought that with all his faults he would never stoop to anything petty, but this sudden resumption of his full authority over her was revengeful. It almost argued that he, too, was hurt—but that was nonsense.

Babette was astounded when she walked in. 'I thought you were at Le Blason!' she exclaimed.

'So I was until nine o'clock this morning.'

'Have you come to collect something?'

'Quite the reverse. I've been collected and brought back.'

'By *le patron*?'

'No. I think he came back last night. I got my instructions this morning.'

'Oh?' Babette said, on an inflection of inquiry. 'Trouble?'

'Not at all. Monsieur Pagel felt we had done the groundwork on the English brochure, so we ought to come back.'

'Sounds like one of his autocratic moods. Ah then, now you're here—I took it upon myself yesterday to ring Edouard.'

'Who?'

'Edouard Masagram. You seemed a bit unwilling, so I took my courage in both hands yesterday afternoon and rang him. *He* sounded a bit unwilling—but then he's so very shy, isn't he, Clarissa?'

Clarissa nodded, only half attending. She was busying herself with the work in the in-tray on her desk, but her mind was going over the cold, businesslike instructions she had had from Roland that morning.

'Finally he said he would be delighted to go to the Tchaikovsky concert on Thursday and give me a lift there and back, so now of course since you're here instead of at Vevey, he'll drive you too.'

'Who?' Clarissa asked.

'Edouard—he'll take us to the concert in Montreux.'

'Oh yes. Well, good. That's great.'

'So at lunchtime today let's go and get tickets.'

'Yes, let's.'

In the event Babette was given some urgent work by Madame Gebermann, so Clarissa went on her own to the office in Grand-Passage. She bought tickets for Thursday for Babette, Edouard and herself; then, on browsing through the brochure, discovered that there were to be recitals of music in the Château de Chillon.

The music to be performed was chamber music, that highly specialised and intellectual music where only a few performers are involved. Clarissa had never been to a recital of chamber music and didn't know whether she would like it, but she very much wanted to go inside the Château de Chillon at night.

Because she loved poetry, Clarissa had read of Chillon in the works of Byron. The champion of Swiss liberty, François Bonivard, had been penned up in the dungeons there during the early days of the sixteenth century, inspiring Byron to write:

Chillon! thy prison is a holy place,
And thy sad floor an altar, for 'twas trod
Until his very steps have left a trace . . .

From the mountains above Vevey and Montreux one could look down and see the castle jutting into the lake, its honey-coloured walls reflected in the silver-blue waters. Once it had been an awesome place, for four years the prison of the great Swiss leader and a fortress of impregnable power. Now it was simply a very beautiful old building, open to the public who could see the very pillar in the vaults to which Bonivard had been chained.

Though Clarissa had often glimpsed it and admired it, she had never been inside it—partly because she didn't much enjoy going round with a group of chattering tourists who would destroy the atmosphere of the place. But to go at night, when few people would be present and the pure, disembodied music would drift in the stillness—*that* would be something.

Since she was pretty sure Babette wouldn't care for

it—and besides, the tickets were expensive—she booked for herself alone.

When she got back to the office she found Babette engaged on a telephone conversation. She looked up as Clarissa came in, pointed at the receiver, and mouthed: 'Edouard!'

'It's so kind of you,' she said into the phone. 'It makes such a difference ... Yes ... Yes ... She's here now.' She signalled to Clarissa. 'He wants to know if you got the tickets?'

'Yes, three in Row Twenty.'

'Three in Row Twenty,' Babette repeated to Edouard. 'Yes. Eight-fifteen, I think. Clarissa, what time does the concert begin?'

Clarissa ranged the three tickets in front of her, so that she could have all the information she wanted, then went to her desk. She ceased to give her attention to the other girl until suddenly Babette said: 'Do you want to speak to her?'

She couldn't do anything else but take the instrument from her. 'Hello, Edouard,' she said.

'Hello, Clarissa. I th-thought you were to be at Le Blason for some time?'

'No, I came back this morning.'

She could almost hear Edouard trying to work out what this sudden return might mean.

'It's very kind of you to provide transport,' she said.

'It should be a good concert.'

'Yes, indeed. I'll see you on Thursday, then?'

'Yes, I'm picking up Babette about six o'clock. I should be at your door about ten past.'

'I'll be ready.'

There had been a slight constraint in his manner, which was still there on Thursday evening when she stepped out of the hallway to greet him. But everything worked out rather well. Because he had picked up Babette first it seemed only natural that she should sit in front with him, while Clarissa sat in the back. All the way along the auto-route Babette kept up a constant bright chatter to which Clarissa needed to contribute only an occasional remark.

125

As they came through Vevey, a turn in the coastline gave Clarissa a view of the floodlit Château de Chillon, tiny in the distance beyond Montreux but perfect against the purple velvet of the night-shadowed lake. The recital was next Monday. It suddenly occurred to her to wonder what she would do for transport on Monday night. She would have to come by train to Montreux and then by trolley-bus to Chillon—and since the ticket had 'Gala' printed on it she would have to wear a long dress, so wasn't she going to look rather silly?

It was as well that they were early at the concert hall, for parking was a considerable problem. Young police-men with illuminated batons waved directions, cars queued up, and Edouard got flustered. But by and by he had put the Passat where the traffic-policemen instructed. They made their way along the *quai*; in front of the Maison des Congrès, swans moved mysteriously on a lake surface like polished black glass.

As always, Clarissa was struck by the formality and elegance of the people going into the foyer. The Swiss made an occasion of everything, and dressed up for it. Whereas in London you could saunter into the Festival Hall in slacks and a sweater and not be noticed, here it would be frowned upon: the concertgoers felt that the new Maison des Congrès deserved the compliment of evening clothes.

But Clarissa and Babette didn't disgrace the occasion. Clarissa was wearing her long brown cotton dress with a tiger's-eye brooch at the centre of the neckline. Round her throat she had a single strand of fine gold-coloured chain. Babette was somewhat more luxurious, in pink and white silk with a billowy skirt and some very real-looking pearls. Their escort was in a rather old-fashioned evening jacket which looked as if it might date from his graduation ceremony.

They bought programmes and tickets for coffee at the interval, then settled themselves. Babette explained earnestly that she adored Tchaikovsky, had recordings of all his ballet music, had seen and adored 'Eugène Onegin' and had hated the film about his marriage.

Edouard said: 'I agree,' 'Oh yes!' and 'Really?' Clarissa amused herself watching the arrival of the rich concert-goers who had the really expensive seats at the front of the hall.

For a moment the amusement died as she saw Gottfried Zucher, her dinner partner of the previous Saturday, followed by his wife and a girl of about nineteen who was a younger version of Madame Zucher. Bringing up the rear was Roland Pagel.

Clarissa had not so much as glimpsed him at the office, although his presence made itself felt by the pressure of work. She watched as he followed to the front of the parterre; he settled the ladies and then sat down, but she could still see him occasionally as he leaned across to listen to something Mademoiselle Zucher was saying. He was very distinguished in his dark blue evening jacket, which acted as a foil to Mademoiselle Zucher's dress of gold tissue.

When the concert began it was some minutes before Clarissa could make herself concentrate on the music. But the second item was the piano concerto, played by a famous soloist, and after the opening bars she was lost to the world. The music, opulent and colourful, reverberated from the warm reflecting copper on the walls of the concert hall, a sea of sound that swept all before it.

With a start she returned to ordinary life as the last chords died away and a roar of applause rang out. Babette was demanding to know if she'd enjoyed it, and wasn't it hot, and would she like coffee or fruit juice?

Edouard went off to fetch the refreshments. The whole audience poured out into the big ante-room, to meet and greet each other and discuss the performance.

'Ah, little white dove!' boomed a voice. 'Tonight you are transformed into a little brown linnet.'

She turned to meet the warm handshake of Gottfried Zucher. 'How are you, *monsieur?*'

'Bored, my dear. I hate this solemn stuff, but my wife, you know . . .' He shrugged expressively. His wife appeared at his side and he broke off abruptly. 'Do you see, Minna? It's Rollé's little secretary. Rollé! Rollé!'

Roland was at the bar, ordering champagne. He glanced over his shoulder at Gottfried's imperious call, and made his way towards him holding two glasses shoulder-high to avoid the crush. It was only as he was almost upon them that he saw Clarissa.

'Your little secretary, Roland,' said Madame Zucher. Roland inclined his head. Clarissa gave a small, polite nod.

'Will you have some champagne?' Gottfried said, taking a glass from Roland to hand to her.

'Oh ... no, thank you, Monsieur Zucher, someone's getting me a drink.' She gave him a little bow and edged away into the crowd, towards the coffee bar. She thought that Madame Zucher wasn't displeased to see her go, and suddenly realised that to mothers of unmarried daughters, Roland Pagel must be a target for matrimony. No doubt it was at her invitation he was here tonight, in the company of young Mademoiselle Zucher.

She found Babette waiting for her in a comfortable corner formed by a low glass table and a white leather bench. 'That was G. G. Zucher, the financier, who shook hands with you, wasn't it?' she asked in a tone of awe.

'Yes, I met him at a dinner party at Le Blason.'

'Good gracious, Clarissa, you say it so calmly! Don't you realise that in all the time Madame Gebermann has been working for *le patron*, she's never been invited to a party at Le Blason?'

All at once it came back into Clarissa's mind that Roland said he could easily arrange for her to meet important people, since she was ambitious. And though there had been a coolness between them at the time because of Jean-Louis, he had nevertheless invited her to the dinner. She saw now that it would really have been quite easy for him to fill her place at table—his circle of acquaintances was enormous and there must be a dozen women who would have been pleased to accept even at short notice.

What a strange unfathomable man! She was still puzzling over the thought when Edouard arrived with the coffee. 'I saw you talking to Roland,' he remarked in a rather accusatory voice.

'In fact she was talking to G. G. Zucher, Edouard,' Babette broke in, eager to name-drop. 'Monsieur Pagel hardly spoke to you, Clarissa, did he?' She was struck by a thought. 'He's still in a bad mood with you, obviously.'

Edouard looked his question. Babette began, 'Oh, sent back in disgrace on Monday—' but Clarissa stopped her with a hand on her arm.

'That's enough, Babette.' She gave Edouard a momentary glance. 'There have been quite enough wrong impressions, one way and another. Tell me, Edouard, what did you think of the pianist?'

Their musical criticisms lasted until the chime sounded to summon them back to their places. The second half of the programme was the strange, sinister and exotic fifth Symphony of Tchaikovsky: usually Clarissa found it overpowering. But tonight the stormy waves of emotion washed over her, yet left her unmoved. She was unable to surrender to it. It was as if her heart was already too full of her own cares for the remembered tragedy of a nineteenth-century Russian to touch her.

Before her eyes a picture formed and re-formed: Roland a moment ago, inclining his head with icy politeness, while superimposed upon it and blotting it out there came the memory of his expression as he raised his head after slipping her sandal back on her foot.

'Never fear, Cendrillon, your prince has found your slipper. . . .'

She closed her eyes so as to close out the picture. He was not her prince. The old legend had no aptness to her story. She wouldn't let herself think about it any more.

But oh, it hurt to have him treat her with so much coldness!

The following day Clarissa had a little conference with Madame Gebermann about the problem of getting back from the Château de Chillon concert in time for work on Tuesday morning. Inquiries had shown that she was unlikely to get back from the castle to Montreux in time to catch the Geneva train, which left about eleven o'clock; even if she caught it she wouldn't be indoors before midnight, after spending about three hours travelling. Besides, she really didn't want to travel wearing an evening dress and evening shoes. She could of course hire a car, but once again that condemned her to something of an ordeal—getting out of a parking lot unknown to her, at night, and with a two-hour drive ahead of her in the dark.

Her solution was to take a hotel room in Montreux for the night. This would enable her to take her dress in an overnight bag, shower and change at leisure in time for the recital at nine-fifteen p.m., and then come back to a light meal in the hotel coffee-shop and a good night's rest. If she could get the day off on Tuesday, she intended to spend it exploring old Montreux, the part of the town which clothed the slope of the mountain away from the lakeshore and all its holiday glitter. Above it lay country roads and mountain paths that she had often wanted to wander on.

Madame Gebermann had no interest in music, scarcely knew that there was a Music Festival on in Montreux, and marvelled that anyone should go to such trouble to attend a concert. But when she heard how much Clarissa had paid for her ticket, her thrifty Genevese soul was filled with concern that Clarissa should get full value for it. Moreover Clarissa had worked well, clearing the backlog of the English correspondence, handling the translation of the handbook, emptying the in-tray . . . Always punctual, always dependable, and apparently able to stand up to Monsieur Pagel's autocratic manner in a way that none of her predecessors had done. . . .

'Very well, you may have Tuesday off. It fits in very well, Mademoiselle Oakley, because it so happens that Monsieur Pagel is not coming into the office on either Monday or Tuesday, so you will not be required.'

'Thank you, Madame Gebermann.'

Over the weekend Clarissa surveyed her wardrobe and tried to make up her mind which dress to take for the recital. The marvellously warm fine weather was holding although they were into the second week of September; she would wear her white dress, which might not get many more airings as the winter drew on. For Tuesday, which she had decided to make an open-air day, she would take her blue and white cotton dress.

With it she usually wore ear-clips of pale blue porcelain. She opened the drawer to find them—and there, carefully wrapped in a tissue, was the little nosegay of cornflowers that Roland had bought her the evening he took her to the wine-cellar.

Lifting them out, she unfolded the tissue. The blue petals had faded almost to grey; as she touched them the flowers fell apart.

With a little grimace she swept the whole thing off her dressing-table and into the wastepaper-basket. What a fool to keep them! What had she been commemorating? An evening at a *cave folkloristique*, the first step in a campaign to let her know he was interested . . . Had she really imagined she was the first? The locale would vary, of course—a more sophisticated girl would be taken to a disco, a connoisseur of the good life to a great restaurant. Because he had detected in Clarissa a romantic who had a weakness for old and legendary things, he had taken her to an old-time wine-cellar, and given her country flowers.

She had chosen the Hotel Suisse in Montreux because it was just across the street from the station. She arrived about six-thirty on Monday evening, had a leisurely bath and a rest, then took her time about dressing. She had no particular reason for making a good effect—no one to impress. She simply wanted to live up to the noble architecture of the château. The white dress looked well. She had no flowers to place at the throat this evening, so instead she pinned there a little brooch she had had since childhood, a tiny wreath of silver leaves, and matched it with little silver clips in her ears.

On her way down to dinner in the restaurant she ordered a taxi for eight-thirty. She ate out on the terrace looking down on to the main street of Montreux with its chains of coloured lights and the Lake of Geneva beyond. A lake steamer went by on its last trip of the day, a blaze of illumination quickly gone; the music from the hotel lounge drifted out into the cool darkness, the scent of the late roses filled the air. Clarissa felt a melancholy peace pervading her.

As her taxi drew up at the Château de Chillon she saw that she was among the first to arrive. The discreet floodlighting threw the building into relief against the night sky and made the moat around it seem deep and sombre. She went across the drawbridge, was ushered onward down an incline of uneven cobbles, and through an ante-room that brought to her mind the vestry of the old parish church at home.

But then she came into the recital room, a vast stone chamber whose walls were painted in an ancient chevron pattern of black and white. Candles glimmered on the sills of the shuttered windows. Wooden benches were ranged on three sides of the performers' dais, which stood in front of a massive stone fireplace. Already some half a dozen members of the audience had arrived and were sitting patiently, but Clarissa saw on glancing at her watch that there was still quite some time before the beginning of the concert. She went out again, to stroll on under a wide arch into a courtyard. A half-moon was riding in the sky above, sending down a soft, silvery light; she suddenly thought: 'The lake must look wonderful under the moon,' and made her way up a flight of stone stairs to what she hoped would be a viewpoint.

She had made her way to the keep of the castle, and true enough, the view was superb. The Alps shone in the faint clear light, the lake shimmered, and those heart-rending beautiful bouquets of spangled radiance that were the lakeside towns were spread out for her to see. Somehow it all chimed in with the vaguely wistful mood that had possessed her since dinner.

But the mood was banished by an extremely practical urge to get back to the recital chamber when from somewhere far away she heard a clock strike the quarter. Quarter past nine! The concert would be starting! She must hurry or she would miss the first item.

Well, it proved easier said than done. Hurrying in the dark in a medieval castle isn't to be recommended. There were arches and passages—and surely she had been facing north when she first came through the main entrance?

It took her ten minutes of stumbling over the uneven stones in an increasing panic before she at last came to a thick oaken door which opened when she twisted the handle. At the other end of a flagstoned passage she could hear the noise of conversation. She hurried towards it. At last—the recital hall.

But what a crowd! When she first arrived there had been seven people including herself. Now there seemed to be hundreds, packed on the fine old oak benches and with not a place to spare. Many were already standing at the side by the door.

Clarissa presented her ticket. The young man acting as usher studied it helplessly and gestured towards the centre of a crowded area on the left. 'Your place should be there, *mademoiselle*, but as you can see . . .'

It appeared the usually efficient Swiss had over-estimated the seating capacity of the room. There was no space for Clarissa nor for the ten or twelve others who were also armed with tickets, and so great was the muddle that the recital couldn't begin.

Clarissa was tremendously disappointed. Somehow she had imagined an occasion of slow-moving elegance, with the musicians performing before an élite group numbering a dozen or two. This rather cramped and uncomfortable gathering had never occurred to her. Shaking her head, she was turning away in hopes of getting outside in time to grab one of the taxis that had presumably brought other concertgoers. But then a familiar voice made her pause.

On the far side of the room Roland had just come in. He was speaking to an elderly man who, like himself, wore the colours of the Vaud canton on the lapel of his evening jacket, and in the rapid dialect French which she occasionally heard among the country people.

As he saw her he broke off in mid-sentence. His companion went on with the discussion; Roland cut him short with a little shake of the head, stooped for a moment to speak to a grey-haired lady perched uncomfortably on the end of a bench in the third row, and then with difficulty made his way round the front of the audience to Clarissa.

'You're here for the recital?'

She nodded. 'I'd no idea there would be so many people.'

'There's been a slip-up, I'm afraid. Laplanche is having some extra chairs brought in—ah, here they are.'

Various young helpers appeared carrying chairs clearly filched from other parts of the castle.

'Excuse me,' Roland said, and re-crossed the room.

Clarissa watched him. The seats were set out. He helped the grey-haired lady from her place on the bench to the more comfortable haven of a straight-backed chair, then came back holding another over his head.

'There,' he said, setting it down by Clarissa. 'Sit down.'

She obeyed gladly. Somehow all except two of the unlucky ones were found a place to sit, and after fifteen minutes' delay the performers filed in.

The whole evening was totally at variance with what Clarissa had expected. She knew she was lucky to be sitting down, but the chair was terribly uncomfortable. The room, though impressive, was draughty. The acoustics weren't good. The audience tried to be appreciative, but in the circumstances it was difficult. Delicate works by Mozart and Vivaldi weren't really equal to the spartan surroundings, and when after the first two items there was an interval of ten minutes, Clarissa decided she had had enough. Nor was she the only one. A young married couple came out at the same time and, seeing she had no transport, gave her a lift back to Montreux.

And so ended the candlelit evening that she had so looked forward to and idealised in her mind.

All the same Clarissa rose early next morning in a mood of renewed optimism. She had the whole day ahead of her to use as she pleased. The haze on Lake Geneva heralded another hot day, so the best thing was to go out early and while it was still cool, work her way up into the mountains so that by midday she would be up where the breeze was blowing.

She put on her blue cotton dress and a pair of casual suède shoes with good thick soles. Her hair was tied back in a blue silk headscarf; she clipped on the blue ear-rings and tucked sunglasses into her shoulder-bag. Reflecting that the Swiss habit of early rising certainly paid dividends, she was out and on her way by eight o'clock.

She took the bus to the Place des Planches, the centre of the strange little confusion of old houses, studios, antique shops and galleries that made up the original town of Montreux. From there she wandered up and down for an hour or more, greatly tempted to buy something from Haldy's marvellous collection of rural working tools but unwilling to burden herself with parcels so early in the day.

Around ten-thirty she had coffee at the Hotel de l'Union, then set off up the steep slope almost opposite. This was an alley she had glimpsed on a previous visit, the Ruelle du Chaudron, which led by steps to a mountain path signposted as a walkers' route. She paused to consider: should she go left to the Gorge du Chaudron and Glion, or right to Caux and the Col de Jaman? The Col was too far—three and a quarter hours, the signpost announced, and that meant for serious walkers who kept up a good pace. Clarissa, on her leisurely way, would be far better to head for Glion, from which she could take the mountain-train back after lunch.

So she went on to the left, up the narrow path, past first one chalet and then another, over the narrow bridge across the gorge where the view might have been beautiful if the great buttresses of the auto-route had not spoiled it. Soon she had climbed the far slope and was leaving it behind. She came out on a level with the auto-route, crossed it, and went on up a quiet road; when she looked back she could see the last of the houses of the old town and the spire of the Eglise de Montreux.

There was a row of dwellings here, a postbox, a café, and a fountain gushing with the cold grey water of the mountains. She paused to let the freshness pour over her hands and wrists. A lad in breeches and short jacket came up with a stoppered jug to fill; she had learned that the water was prized for its mineral properties. He said a shy, 'B'jou', m'selle' and eyed her covertly as he let the stream from the spout splash into the bottle.

A moment later someone came up behind Clarissa. The boy said, 'B'jou', M'sieur Rollé,' nodded, put the stopper in his bottle and walked away. Clarissa turned her head idly.

There, filling a tooled copper jug at the fountain, was Roland.

Utter astonishment held them both silent for perhaps three full seconds. Then Roland realised that the fountain was gushing not into the jug but all over it: he steadied his hand.

'What are you doing here?' he demanded, giving his attention to his task.

'Exploring. I stayed overnight in a hotel down there' —Clarissa nodded down towards the lakeshore— 'because I didn't think I'd make it to the station in time for the last train. Madame Gebermann allowed me a day off.'

'You didn't stay till the end last night.' He set the copper jug on the edge of the trough of the fountain.

'No, it was so desperately uncomfortable.'

'I looked for you to offer you a lift afterwards.'

'That was kind of you.' She was looking down, fiddling with her folded sunglasses. She was burning to ask what *he* was doing here. He was wearing dark blue slacks and a short-sleeved shirt; he was more like the man she had first seen on that early morning in Geneva, driving a dump-truck. The cold, calculating Roland Pagel of the Geneva office building seemed far away.

She had a feeling he was studying her as she sat with her head bent. Presumably he was trying to think of a way to say goodbye and get rid of her. For all at once it rushed upon her: what else would he be doing in this quiet district of old Montreux except visiting the mysterious woman friend?

He said: 'Are you heading anywhere in particular?'

'I thought of walking to Glion.'

'Could you give me a few minutes of your time? There's someone I should like you to meet.'

Clarissa said: 'Yes,' on a gasp of surprise that she was sure would strike him as odd. But he gave no sign. He made a little gesture of invitation, picked up the ewer of mineral water, and led the way.

Behind the row of three-storey village dwellings was a lane. Clarissa saw that the little green saloon car from Le Blason was parked there. To her surprise Roland paused at the ground floor front door of one of the apartments. She had expected him to take her to some much grander house.

He turned the handle and went in, calling out in the rural dialect that Clarissa could not follow. They were in a simple living-room, rather old-fashioned but lovingly cared for. Beyond, through an open door, was a kitchen, from which came the fragrance of freshly-brewed coffee. Someone set down a metal dish and came to the door.

'This is Mademoiselle Oakley, the English girl I mentioned, Maman. Clarissa, may I introduce my mother?'

CHAPTER VIII

Clarissa drew in a sharp breath, but managed to say, '*Enchantée, madame.*'

The woman coming out of the kitchen was small, rather thin, and grey-haired. She had spectacles with very strong lenses, which gave her a lost and inquiring look. Though she was now wearing a grey dress and a floral-embroidered apron, Clarissa had no difficulty in recognising the lady for whom Roland had obtained a chair last night.

'Good morning, Mademoiselle Oakley,' she murmured, peering at Clarissa. 'That was you last night, was it? In the white dress?'

'Yes, *madame*. Did you enjoy the recital?'

'So much! Did you?'

'I'm afraid not. I left at the interval because I

found the chairs too hard.'

Madame Pagel smiled. 'Ah, you young ones! That doesn't perturb me, you see. I was brought up to the simple life.' She nodded at a chair. 'Sit down, *mademoiselle*. Will you take some coffee?'

'Well ... I had some half an hour ago. . . .' But from behind his mother Roland was nodding at her, so she ended, 'All the same it smells so good, I must accept.'

'I'll get it,' Roland said.

'No, no. Please to keep out of my kitchen, Rollé!' She took the pitcher of mineral water from him and went back with a light, uneven step to her stove.

'She likes to do everything herself,' Roland explained in a low voice, 'but she can scarcely see her own hand in front of her face. If she spills the coffee, perhaps you won't . . .?'

'Of course not,' Clarissa agreed swiftly.

From beyond the doorway came the chink of cups, the clink of spoons. After a moment Madame Pagel came back carrying a tray. Clarissa noticed that some slight awkwardness of her arm was making everything on it tilt slowly to the left. Roland took it from her and set it on a table near the window, but not in time to prevent coffee tipping from the pot and cream from the jug.

But his mother managed the filling of the cups quite well. The coffee was delicious.

'You're one of my son's secretaries, I believe,' she remarked.

'Yes, *madame*. I deal with the English correspondence.'

'Are you enjoying the work?'

'Very much indeed.'

'I wonder at that. *I* shouldn't like to work in a city.'

'But it's so beautiful, *madame*. The lake is superb.'

'Yes.' She hesitated, seemed to search for another topic, but failed to find one.

'I met Clarissa quite by chance,' Roland said. 'She was by the fountain.'

'Oh yes.' Helped by this hint, his mother said, 'Rollé always fetches me some spring water when he calls on me. I like to drink it with my meals.' Having said this, she seemed to realise that it was not much help to the conversation, so added awkwardly: 'Do you have mineral streams in London?'

Her son smiled and frowned, amused at the remark but fearful that Clarissa would laugh. Clarissa, however, said in a regretful tone: 'I'm afraid London has very few streams, and none of them are suitable for drinking. You're so lucky here.'

'*N'est-ce pas!*' agreed Madame Pagel. 'It's as I said. I can't imagine anyone being happy in a city.' She cast a vague affectionate glance towards her son. '*Tu vois*, Rollé? It is much better to live here in the Vaud, where everything is fresh and good.'

'You're quite right, Maman. I long ago gave up trying to argue with you on that point.'

Clarissa remarked that the view from the window was very lovely. The old lady said eagerly: 'Can you see the spire? When I was first married I used to sit here with my embroidery, and watch the sunlight glinting on the spire.'

'It's looking its best today.'

She smiled at the reply and nodded in silence. After that she contributed almost nothing to the conversation until Clarissa said she thought she ought to go.

'Can I give you a lift anywhere?' Roland inquired.

'Thank you, but I'm really out for the walk.'

'Take her up to Toveyre,' said Madame Pagel. 'That was always your father's favourite walk. Goodbye, *mademoiselle*, I hope we meet again.'

Roland accompanied Clarissa outside. 'Would you like to go up to Toveyre?' he inquired. · 'It's a steep walk, and perhaps you'd find it too much . . .'

Clarissa said impulsively, 'I should love to.'

'If you'd allow me, I could offer you lunch there and then when we come down again I could drive you back to your hotel in Montreux.'

'Thank you.' They fell into step. After a moment she said, 'What happened to your mother's eyesight?'

'It happened years ago. She was out walking in the mountains with my father and she had a fall. Nothing serious, it seemed at the time. But she damaged some of the nerve cells. It's gradually been getting worse ever since. For the same reason—did you notice?—her sense of balance is poor.'

'She manages very well, though.'

'I suppose so. She's very stubborn. . . . She ought not to live alone, really.'

'She's a widow?'

'Yes, my father died fifteen years ago. He was a woodworker—what do you say in English? *Ebéniste?*'

'Cabinet-maker.'

'*C'est ça.* He had a small business of his own, nothing much.' He smiled in reminiscence. 'It was from him that I first learnt to use tools. He was expert in working with panelling—many of the fine houses in these mountains have rooms lined with his handiwork. But he was content with that. . . .'

'With working in other people's houses, you mean?'

'Exactly so. For me that became intolerable. I wanted to do something better—to *be* someone. He never understood. He was content to go on for ever, putting his ability to work for other men.'

'I know exactly what you mean. My family are like that too.'

'Your family. They are in England, of course.'

'In the North of England. They seemed to think I was mad to want to do anything different.'

'You are friends with them still, however?'

'Oh yes. Yes, of course.' She looked at him in surprise. 'We write to each other regularly.'

They paused by a curve in the lane, to look over a low stone wall at the vine-covered slopes below. A little grey-green lizard scuttled into a crevice between the stones. Roland stared down, but his eyes didn't take in the view.

'I quarrelled with my father. I was bad-tempered, impatient . . .' He moved his shoulders ruefully. 'Well, I have not changed much. So we were not friends when I left my home. I did not tell them where I went, I did not write my address to them. So for more than four years we lost touch completely. I was too proud, you see, to contact them until I could show my father that I had made more success than he had.'

'But you wrote to them at last.'

'I came back. A brand new car, money in my pockets . . .'

'To make your father proud of you?'

'To show him how wrong he had been. But I was too late. He had died during the previous winter.'

'Oh, *Roland* . . .'

He looked at her. 'You say that as if it makes you sad. It made *me* sad, Clarissa. I could not forgive myself. I wanted to make it up to my mother—to prove to her that though I had neglected her, I loved her. But she will take nothing from me.'

Clarissa nodded. 'You said she was stubborn.'

'Stubborn, and proud. The more money I make, the less it interests her. I have asked her a thousand times to come and live with me, but no—she is sure she wouldn't like it. She is sure she would be a handicap to me. She gets tongue-tied, she is short-sighted, she knocks things over, she doesn't like cities or the people who rush about in them. So what can I do?'

'You do what you can. You visit her often.'

'Oh, that's so little.' Then he gave her a sidelong glance. 'Of course I know it causes the gossip to ripple up and down the shores of Lac Leman.'

She knew the colour rose in her cheeks.

'Ah, so you have heard the rumours.' He was ironically amused.

'But Roland, if you know what people are saying, why don't you explain?'

'Explain? I have nothing to explain! And in any case to do so would make people aware of my mother's existence. You must know, Clarissa, that there are people who would imagine they could influence me by influencing my mother—she would have no peace. And if she wants to live in seclusion, in my view she is entitled.'

She could only nod acknowledgment of his reasoning. She couldn't confess to him how much the gossip had distressed her.

'Besides,' Roland added with cynicism, 'for a confirmed bachelor like myself, the rumour that I'm involved in a long-standing and secret *amour* is quite a good safeguard.'

She knew that was true. Simone Masagram regarded her own chances as weakened by the claims of this mythical 'other woman'.

'Have you never been in love, Roland?' she murmured.

She stole a glance at him as he replied. His face was like granite. 'Too busy,' he said. 'I haven't time to waste on emotion.'

There was no more to be said. When he strode on up the steep path, Clarissa followed in silence.

As they came up to the rocks at Toveyre, he turned and pointed to the top of the ravine further up the shoulder of the mountain. 'I was over there yesterday,' he said. 'Spent all day there.'

'Climbing?'

'Good heavens, no. There's a ski hotel going up there beginning next spring. I was having a look at a route for the equipment to go up.'

She shaded her eyes and stared across at the edge of rock. 'Is there a road?'

'Not much of a road at present, but we can improve it once we get the go-ahead. Just at the moment I'm arranging to have some stuff hoisted up by engineer's pulley.'

She tried to focus on a line of thin black, like twine. 'There's a *téléférique*, isn't there? Can't you use that?'

'Only for small packages, and at specified times. And once the snow comes the skiers will monopolise it completely. At the moment we utilise it when the passenger load is low, or during official maintenance sessions. It allows us to get hand tools and such things as wheelbarrows up to the top.'

'It's a marvellous site,' Clarissa observed. 'Who's putting up the money?

'The Chaval chain. Simone is already getting some publicity together for the holiday firms to let them know what sort of package-deal skiing they can expect up there the winter after next.'

Clarissa reflected how far ahead one had to look in business. The hotel had not even been begun yet; indeed, the equipment to build it couldn't yet be winched up to the cliff top. But Simone was already sending out information so that holidaymakers could begin to think about coming here for a stay in eighteen months' time.

They went on up the track. The going was not particularly bad underfoot, but the way was narrow and steep, so that they had to go in single file, thus precluding conversation.

Toveyre turned out to be a few houses and a stop on the MGL mountain railway, scarcely more. The main road went over the precipitous railway line and the track on which Clarissa and Roland had been walking joined it here. There was no restaurant in sight, but Roland led the way on up the road to where the Auberge Belle Terrasse welcomed them.

It was a simple place, patronised by walkers and climbers rather than passing motorists; a trio of workmen were eating their own food, helped out by the local wine from the inn cellar. Roland paused a moment to speak to them after he had escorted Clarissa to a table, and when he rejoined her remarked that they were engineers employed on maintenance of the rail system.

'I did some of that, you know,' he continued. 'It taught me a lot. There's nothing we Swiss don't know about getting people and things up mountains!'

She could tell that his thoughts were preoccupied with the work to be done on the far side of the ravine for the new hotel, and realised how difficult it must be for his mother to have anything in common with this man. His mind and energies were given to topics far outside her ken; his leisure hours, few as they were, were spent with people when she could never understand. Clarissa felt that he really needed a wife—to cope with the social side, to preside over his entertaining, to share his problems and cushion him from minor irritations.

Someone like Simone Masagram, she admitted to herself. Brilliant, capable, completely *au fait* with Swiss society. It was true that Roland had said he had never had time for love, therefore between Simone and himself there was nothing but a business friendship—on *his* side. But to Simone he was more important than a mere business acquaintance; and perhaps for a man like

Roland that would be an ideal solution—a wife who adored him without expecting love in return. A wife like Simone.

'Or like me!' cried some inner voice. But she made herself deaf to the words. It was useless, senseless, to think such things. She had heard Roland's views from his own mouth—he found her attractive, yes, but it wasn't love because he 'hadn't time to waste on emotion'. Even though she had learned there was no prior claim on him—no mysterious 'lady at Montreux' who held him captive in love—it made no difference.

The meal was brought in an unhurried fashion quite different from the bustling restaurants of the cities. First home-made pâté, then fresh fish from the local stream followed by veal in a cream sauce. The waitress paused for long discussions of what vegetables to bring, or whether rye bread would be better than a *brioche*. Two hours later they emerged from the inn, relaxed and contented.

'I ought to spend more time up here,' Roland remarked. 'I feel at home here. . . . But that's what I always say, and one hour after I get back to the office I've forgotten it.'

'I like it here,' Clarissa agreed. 'I'm so glad you brought me.'

'Are you?' He hesitated as if about to say something, but the trio of workmen came clattering out on their way to resume their track maintenance.

Roland led the way out to the road. 'After that enormous meal, would you prefer to go down to Montreux on the railway?'

'No, no! I must walk off the after-effects!'

He laughed. 'Very well. It's easier going down than coming up, of course, but we'll make a little détour to look at the *téléférique* at Jussaux. That will give me a chance to speak to the station-master.'

His mind was always on business, she thought. Well, why not? One didn't become a millionaire by wasting one's time.

The cable-car station at Jussaux was deserted. Passengers were likely to be few on a working day in mid-September for a service that took the traveller on a seventeen-minute swing across the deep ravine to a precipice on the far side, where at the moment there was nothing but rocks and perhaps a safety hut. But once the snow came, the hourly cable-car would be packed with skiers heading for the steep slopes that went down from La Berlue, the Glittering Rock.

Clarissa sat idly by, watching the two tiny red boxes on the cable pass each other out over the valley. The car approaching Jussaux wound itself in to a humming of the wires and the sound of brake-drums in the terminus. The car-man stepped out, began to set down various packages—postal packages from mountain farms on their way to the mail train down in Montreux. That done, he began to take on board packages awaiting him on the concrete ramp, some square cartons and some irregularly shaped bundles wrapped in black polythene. Clarissa recognised the printing and insignia on the labels—the green and white intertwined initials of Entreprise Pagel. So this was some of the equipment going across for the construction site at La Berlue.

'Would you like to go across?' Roland asked, seeing her shade her eyes to look at the other side.

'Oh no!' she said quickly. She was quite sure the cable-car was safe, but had no desire to go swinging out over hundreds of feet of nothingness unless it was strictly necessary. 'No, Roland, there isn't another car back till an hour hence, in any case.'

'Quite true. We could walk down from La Berlue, but'—with a glance at her feet—'not in those shoes. No, we'd better stick to the more civilised road down to the west of Les Planches and my mother's house. Off we go, then.'

There was no doubt he knew the district like the back of his hand. Clarissa had a sudden picture of him as a boy, roving the mountain tracks and watching the engineers at work on the roads and the railways and the chair lifts, seeing the great ski hotels go up on the slopes, envying the achievements of the builders. Now he was himself someone to be envied—that ambitious boy of thirty years ago.

She felt a great closeness to him. She took his arm as they went down a steep, stepped track and he, imagining she needed to be steadied, pulled her to his side and guided her footsteps. She felt the pull of the muscles in the strong, tanned arm. Her head was against his shoulder so that his face was in profile to her; he was intent on watching the ground ahead of them, the grey-green eyes watchful under the thick straight brows.

Every angle of his features, every aspect, was so inexpressibly dear to her. She was filled with a wild longing to make him stop, to turn him so that he would look deep into her eyes and see the love that was welling there. Perhaps he would respond. Perhaps, in the vast expanse of rock and forest and alpine meadow, they could come face to face as man and woman, as loving and beloved—and he would speak some word of tenderness. . . .

But no. A moment later the seclusion of the path gave place to a more open lane; roofs of houses became visible, she could hear the sound of traffic. A few yards more and they came out on the edge of Les Planches, and from there it was a comfortable stroll up the steep road to the outskirts of Montreux where Madame Pagel lived.

'Should we go in and say "*au revoir*"?' she asked.

'No—I hope she's having her afternoon rest at the moment.' He helped her into the little green Renault, and ten minutes later they were drawing up in the parking area of the Gare de Montreux, opposite Clarissa's hotel.

'What are you doing now?'

'I only have to collect my bag and catch a train back to Geneva,' she explained, with a nod towards the station entrance.

'I'd offer to take you into Geneva, but I have to go back to Le Blason—'

'That's quite all right—I've got a return ticket and it always offends my mercenary soul not to use the return half.'

Laughing, he escorted her across the crossing. 'I'll wait and see you on to the train, at any rate.'

They went into the Hotel Suisse. Clarissa had paid

146

her bill that morning and only had to retrieve her over-night bag from the porter, so she was surprised when the receptionist beckoned to her.

'Mademoiselle Oakley, *n'est-ce pas*?'

'Yes?' She turned to him, Roland at her elbow.

'A gentleman is waiting for you. On the terrace.'

'For me? You must be mistaken.'

'No, it is quite correct.' The clerk consulted a notepad on the counter. 'A Monsieur Blech.'

Surprised and perplexed, Clarissa stepped back. Perhaps she meant to lay a hand on Roland's. But he had already moved away.

'Now I realise I have probably spoiled all your plans for today,' he said, contempt in his voice. 'Even though I *am* your employer, Clarissa, there is no need to give me your free time when you would rather spend it with someone else.'

He was gone before she could speak. In any case, she did not know what explanation to give.

CHAPTER IX

Jean-Louis was sitting against the balustrade of the terrace, a tall glass on the table in front of him. His face lit up as Clarissa walked across the terrace towards him.

'Clarissa! So there you are!'

'Jean-Louis, what on earth are you doing here?'

He had stood up. Now he caught her hand and pulled her down beside him as he resumed his place.

'Clarissa, I've something terribly important to tell you!'

'But how did you know where to find me?'

'I rang your office this morning. Madame What-d'you-call-her told me you'd stayed overnight here at the hotel, so I rang here and they told me they expected you back to collect your luggage by mid-afternoon. So I came.'

'But, Jean-Louis, *why*?'

'I've just made a very important discovery. I'm in love with you.'

'What!'

At that providential moment the waiter arrived. Clarissa ordered the first thing that came into her head, English tea. All she wanted was to get rid of him and be free to tell Jean-Louis not to talk nonsense.

'I know it sounds odd,' he went on as soon as they were alone again. 'I really can't explain why it's taken me so long to understand my—'

'But, Jean-Louis, only about a week ago you were throwing me into Roland's arms and begging me to use my influence with him on your behalf!'

'Don't,' he groaned. 'I know I did. I was so sure I was level-headed and practical that I just wouldn't listen to my own doubts. In any case, my darling, I really didn't see myself standing much of a chance in opposition to Roland Pagel. He could roll over me like a steam-roller if I got in his way.'

'I don't think he would, but—'

'Last night everything was changed. When I heard what you had said—'

'What had I said? What are you talking about?'

'Simone told me. I took her out to dinner—'

'But Jean-Louis,' Clarissa insisted, 'I haven't said anything to Simone! I haven't seen her since a dinner party at Le Blason, over a week ago.'

'Oh, it wasn't what you said to her, it was what you said to Edouard.'

The waiter arrived with the tray to tea. A couple of minutes were occupied while he ranged the cup and the teapot and cream jug before her. Then Clarissa drew a deep breath and made a bid for good sense.

'Begin at the beginning, Jean-Louis,' she prompted, 'otherwise I shall never understand.'

He was about to take her hand, but she busied herself pouring tea. She didn't want any physical contact with him, particularly while he was in this mood of muddled, upsurging emotion.

'Simone and I had dinner last night,' he began. 'She had some instructions for me about publicity photographs. The Chaval Company is going to build a ski-lodge hotel up at La Berlue—oh, you know that?'

'I've just been looking at the place, from the other side of the canyon.'

'What a coincidence! Well, first we talked about that, and whether I should go up there before the snow to do any photography, and then of course, since Entreprise Pagel are the contractors, we began to talk about Roland. Simone seemed a lot less tense and anxious on that score, and when I commented about it she said she'd had some information from Edouard that had put her mind at rest.'

'Edouard? How does Edouard come into it?'

'You went to a concert here with him on Thursday—right?'

'Quite right. With him and Babette Georgeot.'

'And during the interval you happened upon Roland with some of his friends.'

'Yes.' She remembered only too clearly how he had inclined his head to her, refusing to speak.

'Edouard was full of it, according to Simone. Of course the poor chap imagines he's in love with you, but one can't take it seriously—'

'Don't speak like that!' Clarissa said in a sharp tone.

'But, Clarissa—! You're not going to say you care about Edouard?' Jean-Louis's face was suddenly tinged with jealousy.

'Not in the way you mean, Jean-Louis. But even if I don't return Edouard's feelings, that's no reason to belittle them. He could be suffering,' she ended sadly, knowing only too well what the suffering could be.

Jean-Louis shifted uncomfortably in his chair. 'Don't let's waste time over Edouard and his misery,' he said. 'I want to talk about *us*—'

'But you were reporting something Edouard was supposed to have said?'

'Oh yes. He told his sister that at the concert Roland didn't want to speak to you, and that Babette said you were in disgrace. Edouard was awfully pleased—apparently he'd been a bit shattered when I warned him off that afternoon at Le Blason.'

'He certainly was! Don't you remember the look on his face when you brought out that awful phrase—"Clarissa is Roland's girl"?'

'Candidly, no. If I'm quite truthful, Clarissa, I didn't take any of it seriously. That schoolboy-knight-errant business—kissing your hand as if you were the Lady Isolde— I just thought ...' He slowed and hesitated. 'Do you know, I believe I was jealous?'

'Of Edouard?'

'Yes, without knowing it.'

'But apparently you weren't jealous of Roland,' she commented drily.

'Well, in fact, I was. But I knew it was no good trying to fight Roland. I mean to say, darling—one doesn't take on a business giant like Roland Pagel.'

Clarissa wanted to say, 'If you were really in love, you would.' But she had a feeling it would be pointless. Jean-Louis' emotions weren't of a kind that she could analyse successfully and, truth to tell, she didn't really want to hear any more. But having, as he felt, discovered true love, he was determined to tell her about it.

'It was the most extraordinary thing,' he went on. 'When I heard Simone saying, with a great deal of satisfaction, that she thought any budding friendship between you and Roland had withered, I felt ... liberated! As if a great burden of regret and resentment had slipped from my shoulders! I thought, "She's free! She's free!" '

'I've always been free,' said Clarissa.

'Yes ... but ...' Jean-Louis ran a finger up and down the edge of the table. 'You know, if Roland had got serious about you, I shouldn't have stood a chance. Now everything's different. Now we can go back to the way things were that sunny morning we first met, when you were just a nice, unimportant girl from England and I was a fellow who helped you keep your balance when you slipped.'

She remained silent.

'Clarissa?' he urged.

With a little reluctant sigh, she spoke. 'I don't think we can go back, Jean-Louis. A lot has happened in the weeks since we met. Even if we did go back—'

'What?'

'We . . .: we were just acquaintances, after all.'

'No, no, Clarissa! We were more than that! After all, you put yourself out to help me—'

'But, Jean-Louis, I didn't! It never occurred to me I had any power to "help you". It was you yourself who made all the efforts—you turned up uninvited to the Confederation Day party, you struck up an acquaintance with Simone. I didn't do anything.'

'It seems to me you did,' he protested. 'From the moment I met you all sorts of things began happening for me. In a way I began to think of you as my lucky star—'

'Who was it who was jeering at Edouard a moment ago, for treating me like the Lady Isolde?'

He coloured. 'Don't tease me. I'm serious, Clarissa. Since last night it's suddenly become clear to me that you could belong to me. I needn't stand by and watch Roland carry you off—I can reach out my hand and hold on to you.'

Very gently she put a finger against his flushed cheek. 'Only if I want you to.'

He sat still and silent. For perhaps the first time since they had met, Jean-Louis looked directly with his black eyes into Clarissa's. Her calm, direct gaze made him flinch away.

'But you *could* fall in love with me,' he said. 'Why not?'

'I don't think so, Jean-Louis.'

'We have such a lot in common, my darling—'

'What makes you think that?'

'What?' He paused. 'Well, Simone says—'

'Listen, my dear,' Clarissa interrupted. 'What Simone says may count for a lot with her father and brother, and with you. But I don't intend to run my life to fall in with Simone's wishes, let's be quite clear about that.'

'All the same, Clarissa, she's a very shrewd woman. And she certainly put it into my head last night that . . . well, that you were fond of me. She said you'd told that to Edouard.'

'That's quite true.'

'So you see!' he cried in triumph. 'That's great! The way I feel for you, Clarissa, is enough to make up for your lack of certainty. I know you'll come to feel as I do, I just *know* it! Oh, Clarissa, you've made me so happy!'

And to the amusement of the other hotel guests at the terrace tables, Jean-Louis threw his arms around her and covered her face with kisses.

Clarissa's embarrassment was so acute that her one thought was escape. She struggled free, saying she must get her luggage and catch her train. But he threw some money on the table for the waiter, and came after her. When she was being handed her overnight bag by the porter, he intercepted, stowing it in his car, and almost forcibly putting her in the passenger seat.

It ended with her allowing him to drive her home to Geneva. Once there he dearly wanted to take her to dinner or to be invited in for a scratch meal, but she pleaded fatigue after a day's walking. There was some attempt on his part to stage a long good night kiss, but Madame Lallais the *concierge* came up with a postal packet, and Jean-Louis admitted defeat.

'*A bientôt, mon amour!*' he called as he went downstairs. 'I'll ring you tomorrow.'

Madame Lallais watched his disappearing figure with good humour. 'So it's "*mon amour*" now,' she observed. 'You young ones! Rushing into marriage after knowing each other a few months!'

'I'm not going to marry Jean-Louis!' Clarissa said hastily.

'No? But he speaks to you as if *he's* going to marry *you*.'

'Yes . . . well . . . it's just another horrible mix-up . . .' To her own horror, Clarissa's voice broke.

'Oh, *ça alors*! What's the matter, little one? Has the young man been quarrelling with you? Ah, wicked lad, to make you cry!'

'No . . . really, Madame Lallais. It's nothing like that. I think I'm just tired.'

'Poor little girl! Such pale cheeks, and the eyes so big! Come, I have a good *longeole* on the stove. We'll have a quiet little supper—'

'Thank you, *madame*, but I'm not hungry—'

'Then come downstairs and have some coffee. Come now—' She took one of Clarissa's hands in both of hers, which were old and cool and comforting. 'Come and sit in my cosy kitchen, and if you want to cry, then old Madame Lallais has a shoulder ready.'

Clarissa had no intention of crying, but the idea of a quiet half-hour with the old lady wasn't unwelcome. They had built up a polite friendship since Clarissa's arrival: Madame took in parcels for her, and sometimes pegged out a drip-dry dress on her clothes line, whereas Clarissa often brought back little items of shopping from the Place du Molard to save the old lady's legs.

They settled in two wooden armchairs with chintz-covered cushions and head-rests. The coffee-pot began to bubble on the hot-plate. Madame Lallais asked if she had enjoyed the recital at the Château de Chillon and chuckled at Clarissa's account of the discomfort. She inquired about the hotel.

'Very comfortable, by contrast.'

'So what did you do today? You spent it with Monsieur Blech?'

'No, no—with Monsieur Pagel.'

'Ah?' Her sharp little button eyes surveyed Clarissa. 'There is a man for you! *Un Vaudois, quoi!* I am Vaudoise, you know.'

'From Monsieur Pagel's district?'

'No, I am from St Cergue, but all the same we speak the same language, he and I. I wish I had had a son like him, but *hélas*, my three children were all girls and I scarcely see them. I don't complain, though. Thanks to Monsieur Pagel's kindness I have this good little job and a roof over my head—'

'You don't mean he hired you personally?'

'Oh no,' said Madame Lallais, shaking her head vigorously, 'it is his property, of course, but he hasn't time to engage every single person who looks after things for him. No. But three years ago, the man who runs the property department—Monsieur Duval, you've met him? No? Oh, well, why should you? I was saying that Monsieur Duval wished to "modernise" all the buildings, by which I mean put post-boxes with locks in the hall, and an inner door with a little microphone so that callers would announce themselves and from upstairs the resident could release the door.'

'Yes, I've seen that.' The new blocks of flats in Geneva were often fitted in this way.

'Thus doing away with the *concièrges*,' Madame Lallais went on. 'So I thought, "*Hé*, should a Vaudoise let herself be extinguished like that?" and I sat down and I wrote a letter to Monsieur Pagel.' Her eyes sparkled. 'I was very rude to him. I expected to be put out of the door next day.'

'He wouldn't do that,' Clarissa said on a note of. protective denial.

'So you know that about him? Ah . . .? Well then, he sent for me. I went—best black dress, marcasite brooch, clean gloves.' She did a little mime to show how spick and span she had looked, and Clarissa gave a little laugh at the thought of this indomitable old lady preparing to go down with all flags flying.

'And what happened?'

'We had a lovely little chat, about the mountains, and the best way to trim vines, and I explained that if this *sacré* Monsieur Duval modernised all the little old apartment buildings I wouldn't be the only widow to lose her home, and the result is here I still am, and Monsieur Pagel gave me his word that no change would be made while I lived. And I think, my dear, that many another old woman like me owes her livelihood to that promise.'

Clarissa's eyes pricked with tears. 'He can be so kind,' she whispered.

Madame Lallais busied herself pouring the coffee into thick pottery beakers. She sighed a little to herself. Perhaps she was glad not to be a young girl any more.

During the ensuing weeks, as October came and went, Lake Geneva showed a different aspect to Clarissa. The long autumn gave way to a series of storms that echoed and re-echoed round the peaks. The surface of the lake was whipped into foam by gales that rushed down the slopes in turbulent attacks. For some days Clarissa was often reminded of Milton's lines:

> ... nor slept the winds
> Within their stony caves, but rushed abroad
> From the four hinges of the world ...

In a way it all formed an apt background to her life, which seemed to be made up of alternative spells of calm and stress. At the office, everything went forward in perfect tranquillity. She and Babette worked in harmony, each engaged on their separate tasks but often consulting each other, sometimes pausing to chat for a moment's relaxation, and two or three days a week lunching together.

Roland was never to be seen. He was away on business in New York, but even when he was in the office his commands were relayed by Madame Gebermann. Even replies to letters, the out-of-the-ordinary letters which he used to dictate personally, now came to Clarissa on a tape for transcription. If she had any query she typed it on a separate sheet and clipped it to the finished letter; Madame Gebermann sometimes handed on instructions for alterations or other comments, but Clarissa was never summoned to Roland's presence and after a time she ceased to expect it.

Perhaps, she told herself, it was all for the best. If he regarded her as destined for Jean-Louis, that made a barrier which was after all only additional to those formed by his wealth, his position, his declared impatience with love and marriage.

Yet that safeguard, Jean-Louis, caused Clarissa a great deal of trouble. He was the kind of man who could convince himself of anything, or so it seemed. A few months ago he was sure Clarissa was meant for Roland, and tried to make capital out of it. Now he was convinced Clarissa would be in love with him 'any moment now', and simply refused to listen to contradiction. She often longed for the resolution, the cruelty, to tell him she would rather not see him again. But he had worked himself up to such a pitch of fervour that it would have shattered him. She hoped that in the course of time he would get bored and frustrated, and take up some new enthusiasm—like a child who, having been denied a special treat or a present, finds that there are compensations elsewhere and that life goes on nevertheless.

She refused as many of his invitations and dates as she could. But it wasn't altogether easy, because he had quickly become accepted as one of the circle of friends she had in common with Babette, so that it was quite natural to find him in a gathering at someone's house, or included in a day spent up on the ski-slopes. To make things more awkward, this group often included Edouard Masagram.

Edouard had developed a strong attachment to Clarissa. It was an attachment she valued, for she had come to the conclusion that no kinder or more sensitive man had ever come her way; she was inwardly convinced that once his first dependence on her had worn off, they would be friends for the rest of their lives. She was sure that he would cease to be dependent on her: it was mere chance that she, Clarissa Oakley, had been the one to see in him the merits that his family ignored.

It could just as easily have been Babette, if Babette had met him first. Clarissa cherished a secret hope that one day Edouard would look beyond herself to Babette, who continually showed an interest in and consideration for Edouard which was more than mere camaraderie.

But still for the moment he still thought of Clarissa as his first real friend, his good angel. And naturally he resented Jean-Louis and his proprietorial air towards her. Babette noticed it.

'The funny thing is,' she remarked, 'Jean-Louis carries on as if Edouard doesn't exist! Sometimes I could shake him, Clarissa!'

'Me too.' They were sitting surrounded by parcels in the café on the top of the Placette department store, drinking coffee to restore their energies for the rest of their shopping. Clarissa was giving a buffet party that evening in her apartment, for which they had been buying supplies of paper cups, serviettes, and drinking straws.

'The difficulty is,' she went on, 'that Jean-Louis judges people by their success in life. He respects Edouard's sister enormously because she holds down a very important job. But Edouard himself seems to Jean-Louis a nonentity—and matters aren't helped by the fact that that's the way Edouard's family treat him.'

'Did you say they're coming this evening?'

'Well, I told Edouard he could bring them, but I doubt if he will.' Clarissa had done this because she rather thought it was time Babette should meet the formidable Simone and the rather alarming Jules Masagram. If Babette was falling in love with Edouard, she might as well see what she was getting herself into. If they didn't come this evening, Clarissa was determined to bring the Masagram father and daughter into Babette's company in some other way, perhaps over the Christmas period.

Christmas, which was a month away, was giving her cause for thought. She felt she ought to go home to spend it with her parents, but she had had so many kind invitations from Swiss friends that she was strongly tempted to stay. About the middle of December festivities began in Geneva with an event called the Escalade; this was in memory of a great event in 1602, when the townsfolk were summoned forth by the tolling of the great bell of Geneva, La Clémence, to meet a midnight attack by the troops of Savoy. From then on there seemed to be a series of evening and weekend parties which she very much wanted to attend.

On the other hand she hadn't seen her family since July. Now and again, in the midst of the emotional tangles of recent weeks, she had found herself longing for her mother's absent-minded kindness and the placid tenor of the life in Northumberland. A few days at home might be a help. ... If nothing else it would provide a good excuse to escape from Jean-Louis, who was urging her to spend Christmas at a fashionable ski resort.

When they had bought all their shopping she and Babette went to her apartment. Babette helped clear the

157

floor for dancing. They set out the food—cold meats, all sorts of savouries, little dishes of vegetables or poultry in aspic, and a huge bowl of fruit salad; the kitchen table groaned under the display, which they covered with a paper tablecloth.

After that they showered and changed. Babette had brought a dark red dress, which complemented her brunette good looks. Clarissa had decided on a long skirt of sherry-coloured velvet and a blouse of coffee-coloured lace. They surveyed each other with satisfaction.

'Not bad, if I do say so myself,' Babette opined. 'But I really must lose some weight. Stop me if you see me eating any of the pastry, Clarissa.'

Clarissa laughed and hugged her. 'You know you'll only say, "Just this one!" '

The bell rang to announce the arrival of the first guest. From then on people arrived at regular intervals until eight o'clock. Clarissa had invited twelve and catered for twenty, knowing that the younger generation in Switzerland were less formal than their elders and wouldn't think twice about bringing along a friend.

Very much to her surprise, when Edouard arrived he had brought his father and sister.

'So charming of you to ask us,' said Jules, glancing about with a rather scornful eye. He clearly felt he was doing her a great favour by coming to her humble abode. 'And these are your . . . um . . . young friends?'

There was no doubt of the difference between him and the other guests; they were wearing casual evening clothes, the men in dark suits or even sweaters and slacks, the girls in a great variety of styles. But Jules Masagram was in evening jacket and black tie.

Simone was even more splendid, in a décolleté dress of stiff emerald green silk. 'You must forgive us, my dear,' she murmured, 'we're really just dropping in. We're going on to the theatre afterwards.'

Clarissa recalled that there was a late-night charity performance tonight at the Conservatoire. The cream of Geneva society would be there. She said, 'It's nice of you to spare me some time,' and ushered them to the

158

sideboard to pour them some wine.

'How are things with you?' Jules inquired politely.

'Excellent, thank you.'

'It seems a long time since last we met. I suppose it was the summer?'

'At Le Blason,' Clarissa rejoined, remembering the day only too well.

'Ah yes! Edouard and I had quite a little tiff afterwards, didn't we, my boy?'

'Oh, don't let's go into that, Papa,' mumbled Edouard.

Clarissa took him by the elbow. 'Would you go and ask Babette to uncover the food in the kitchen, Edouard, and ask people to help themselves?'

He obeyed. His father drifted off to scrutinise Clarissa's bookshelf. Simone sipped her wine and glanced about. 'Isn't Jean-Louis here?'

'He's coming later. He had an assignment that took him to Berne—'

'Oh yes, I recall that he mentioned it when I last saw him.' She smiled. 'He's a very busy fellow at present, isn't he?'

'Largely thanks to you, I believe, Simone?'

'Oh yes'—negligently—'I've put work his way. Why not? He really is very talented. He's going to do some very useful work for me up at Sparkling Rock.'

'I heard about that.'

'Really? From whom?' Simone looked perplexed. 'I haven't told anyone about it, not even Jean-Louis himself.' Then an expression of recollection came over her face. 'Except . . .'

'Can I refill your glass?'

'No, thank you.'

'Then please come and have something to eat—'

'No, no—Papa and I will be leaving soon. We're being picked up here.'

'What a pity you can't stay,' Clarissa said with complete insincerity.

'You're too kind. Edouard was very keen for us to come—I think he would like us all to become better acquainted for reasons of his own, but, as I pointed out, it's likely to be rather a brief friendship.'

'Really?' Clarissa said, puzzled.

'I suppose you'll be getting married before Jean-Louis makes his big move.'

'Married? But—but I've no plans to get married.'

'Oh, come, my dear, Jean-Louis talks about nothing else. It's quite an open secret, I assure you. He tells me he hopes to have put together enough capital to go abroad by the middle of next year. It's to be Florida, I hear. Shall you like Florida?'

'You must be joking,' Clarissa gasped. 'I'm not going to Florida or anywhere else with Jean-Louis!'

'That's rather inconsiderate, Clarissa. He doesn't really like Switzerland, you know. I gather he finds the winter wearisome. Surely you don't want him to stay here when he'd be happier elsewhere?'

'Simone, I must absolutely insist—'

But the doorbell rang, and she was summoned by those nearest the door to welcome the guest they had just admitted—Jean-Louis himself.

Clarissa took his coat from him, and the bouquet of carnations he had brought. She had intended to be coldly indignant with him, but the moment didn't seem right. She whispered urgently, 'I've got to speak to you, Jean-Louis! Simone's just been telling me your plans— Florida and so forth—'

'Yes, I want to tell you—'

'Ah, Jean-Louis!' cried Monsieur Masagram, happy to meet someone he knew amongst this crowd of nobodies. 'How are you, my dear fellow?'

Jean-Louis looked a little surprised at the cordiality of this greeting from a man who generally treated him as beneath his notice, but replied that he was well and that business was good.

'Yes, yes, so I hear from my daughter. Excellent, excellent—I like to hear of people making their way upward to success.' He glanced angrily across the room at his son, who was handing round plates of food. 'Some young men prefer to let the world pass them by,' he added.

'Oh well, you know, Edouard is different,' Jean-Louis said with a shrug. 'And in any case perhaps he didn't

160

have a goal to aim at. Now *I*, you see, had a goal.' He drew Clarissa's arm through his as he ended.

'So Simone tells me,' her father said. He put a finger to the side of his nose and winked. 'Wedding bells in June, isn't that it?'

'No, no,' Clarissa protested, dragging her arm free. 'You mustn't—'

'Mustn't give away the secret, eh? Very well—silent as the grave. We old diplomats, you know, we can hold our tongues. But next year is going to be a year of change.' He signed. 'I don't really know how I shall manage without Simone.'

'Simone's going away?' said Jean-Louis.

'Well, not very far.' Monsieur Masagram gave a little nod of his silvery-grey head. 'I must take comfort from that. Some daughters, when they marry, go miles away. At least I am spared that.'

'You're—you're speaking of Simone's marriage?' Clarissa said, a terrible fear taking hold of her heart like a giant fist.

'I suppose I ought not to. It's not exactly settled. But I think I know my own daughter well enough to recognise the signs. She keeps telling me I'm not to be afraid of things being different, that I'll get used to it, and that our daily maid has promised to find me a resident housekeeper.'

'The lucky man is Roland, I take it? Jean-Louis asked, although it was hardly a question.

'Who else? It's a good match, of course. They were made for each other.'

'I always thought,' said Clarissa in a husky voice, 'that Roland was a confirmed bachelor?'

'We're all confirmed bachelors until we meet the right girl. I was, until I met you, my darling.' Jean-Louis leaned forward to kiss her lightly on the cheek.

'And then of course there comes a time in a man's career,' added Jules, 'when a wife is a great asset. I remember when I was in the Corps Diplomatique, there came a moment when I took stock and told myself: "I've gone as far as I can in my career as a single man—now I need a wife to share the job." And when you look at

Roland, you know, it's easy to see what a help it would be to have a wife like Simone.'

'Are they actually engaged?'

'Oh, my dear *girl*,' Jules scolded, 'can you imagine the kind of engagement ring Roland will buy for her? It would be impossible not to notice it! No, no, nothing's official yet. Christmas, perhaps—I fancy Simone expects to announce it at Christmas.'

So soon? Clarissa saw the room tilt before her eyes, but drew a deep breath and made it come right again.

If she had heard all this from Simone herself, she might have been able to write it off as wishful thinking. Simone undoubtedly wanted to be Madame Pagel and might have been pleased to have Clarissa believe the marriage would soon take place.

But it was difficult to believe that Simone would have allowed that situation to arise with her father. If she had given her father the impression she would soon be engaged to Roland it was because she thought it would happen.

Why not, indeed? As Jules Masagram said, they were made for each other—she so brilliant, so fashionable and good-looking in her own way; he so successful and influential.

She found herself wondering what Roland's mother would think of her new daughter-in-law. Simone was so exactly what she shrank from—almost the embodiment of the glamour of city life. But then a man doesn't marry to please his mother. And the two women need hardly ever meet: Roland would continue to visit Madame Pagel on his own as he did at present.

How surprised Simone would be when she found out that this rival whom she had resented so much was a short-sighted old lady! Or did she already know? Yes, surely she did. Roland would certainly take the woman he intended to marry to be presented to his mother.

With a pang Clarissa remembered that she had been presented. But that was different! She had stumbled upon the secret: what else could he do except introduce her and ask her not to spread the news, so that his mother's desire for privacy would be respected.

Poor Madame Pagel. She was very unlikely to get on well with Roland's wife. But so long as Roland was happy that was really all that mattered. So Clarissa told herself, as she steeled herself to face the rest of the evening after hearing the news.

Jules Masagram had ended the conversation with the warning, 'Remember, it's still a dark secret. Not a word to anyone.' And so when a moment later chance brought Simone to her side, Clarissa didn't mention the imminent engagement. But she had an idea that Simone had seen her father talking earnestly to their hostess, and guessed what he had been saying.

'I dined at Le Blason last week,' she told Clarissa. 'Albert and his wife asked to be remembered to you.'

'How kind of them! I hope they're well?'

'Quite well. They're a little perturbed at some staff changes that may be coming, but I reassured them. One wouldn't want to part with a good gardener like Albert.'

'Of course not. You ... you take a great interest in ... in the household there.'

'Naturally. Roland has no one else to turn to, and in any case, quite soon—' Simone broke off and shrugged expressively.

'Are you quite sure you won't have something to eat?' Clarissa said, desperate to change the subject.

'No, really, thanks. We ought to have left by now. I can't think where our transport has got to!' Then, as the doorbell sounded, 'Ah, that's probably him.'

Clarissa went to the door. On the threshold stood a man she recognised well—Roland's chauffeur.

'*Bon soir*, Mademoiselle Oakley,' he said, touching his cap. 'Monsieur and Mademoiselle Masagram are ready?'

'We're coming, Georges,' called Simone. She picked her way among the other guests, some of whom were sitting in groups on the floor eating supper, picnic-fashion. The careful way in which she held her skirts clear spoke her opinion of this sort of behaviour.

Her father joined her at the door. 'Well, good night, Clarissa. Thank you for inviting us.' His disdainful glance swept the room. 'Quite delightful,' he said hypocritically, and went out.

'Good night, Clarissa. A charming party. You must let me return your hospitality by coming to us at Christmas.'

'That's awfully kind of you, Simone, but I've decided to go home for Christmas.'

'What a pity. You would have found it interesting, I think. Good night.' She urged her father forward. 'Come along, Papa—we mustn't keep Roland waiting.'

They disappeared down the stairs. Despising herself yet unable to stop herself, Clarissa moved slowly to the landing window and looked out. Below in the lane, the Rolls-Royce was standing. As she watched Jules and his daughter came out of the doorway. A tall figure got out of the Rolls to help Jules in.

The old man settled, Roland turned to give his hand to Simone. She said something and clasped his hand, more as a special greeting than as he had intended it, as an aid to getting into the car.

In return he paused, bowed, and kissed her hand. Clarissa could see the lamplight gleaming on the iron-grey hair at his temples—and then realised that over his bowed head Simone was gazing up at the window.

Dismayed, she moved back. Not for the world would she have Simone know that she had been gazing out of the window. But she knew as she moved that it was too late. Simone had expected her to be there and had seen her witness the meeting with Roland.

Angry with herself, Clarissa went into her apartment and put some loud records of dance music on the record player.

Monday was a bad day. The squally weather had departed, to be replaced by a steady downpour that shrouded Lac Leman in mist. There were a lot of letters in the file handed to her by Madame Gebermann, but they were very dull. Bu midday she had cleared them and after lunch began on those with special instructions.

One of them was a re-type of a letter she had done on Friday from the tape-machine. Clipped to it was a note in Roland's writing: 'You have run two letters into one. Presumably the tape was faulty so that you could not hear where one ended and the other began, but a moment's thought would have shown the error. A little intelligence, please.'

The words blurred in front of Clarissa's eyes. It wasn't so much the irritation expressed, although that hurt. It was the idea of being communicated with by scraps of paper. Was she never to see him again? This man who had held her in his arms and made her blood sing—who had told her he found her attractive—was he to be a clipped voice on a dictation tape, a signature at the end of a letter?

All at once Clarissa knew she couldn't bear any more. All the shining brightness had gone out of her life here on the shores of the shining lake. It was time to go. Away, away from the lovely valley and its city on the silver stretch of water—away from the heartache, away from the unrequited longing. Somewhere in the world was a place for her, where she could forget the tall man who had touched her life with magic.

She rolled paper and carbon into her typewriter and typed rapidly, without stopping to think about style or grammar. She ripped it out of the machine, stood up, and walked out of the office.

'Clarissa—!' Babette exclaimed as she went by, but Clarissa didn't stop to explain.

Outside the door of Madame Gebermann's office she paused to compose herself. Then she walked in quietly and offered the sheet of paper to the private secretary.

'This is my resignation, Madame Gebermann.'

The other woman looked up from her work in dismay. 'Mademoiselle Oakley! Your resignation?' she echoed.

'Yes, madame.'

'But why? It's very sudden!'

'I admit that, but I want you to know I mean it.'

'No, come, mademoiselle—take time to think it over—'

'I don't need to think it over. I've made up my mind.'

'Why? Tell my why! Do you feel overworked?'

'I certainly have plenty to do, but I don't complain of that. I just feel I want to go.'

'Mademoiselle Oakley—Clarissa—please reconsider! I've been so pleased with your work. After so many previous disappointments, I thought that at last I'd got a team together that would endure. What's brought you to this sudden decision?'

'I suppose it is sudden, but the thought has come to me once or twice in the past few weeks—'

'For what reason? Is it anything I have done?'

'Oh no, Madame Gebermann! You're a very considerate senior. No, it's—well, I can't explain.'

'Can't? Or won't?'

Clarissa looked down. 'I'd rather not discuss it. It's a personal matter.'

'Ah,' said Madame Gebermann, sighing, 'I was young once myself, you know. And of course I'm aware that young men ring you here at the office—is it to do with one of them?'

Clarissa clutched at this excuse. 'In a way. There are going to be changes next year, madame, and to stay on here at Entreprise Pagel would not be a good thing.'

'How do you mean?' The older woman couldn't help being curious, and besides, she hoped to find some clue that would clear up the mystery of Clarissa's sudden resignation. 'Who is involved in these changes? Voyons, mademoiselle, if you are thinking of getting married, there is no problem. I am quite prepared to relax the office routine for a while until you learn how to fit in your household chores. Within reason I—'

'I'm not thinking about household chores, madame. I may be leaving Switzerland.'

'Là, là! That is a change indeed! I hadn't realised—'

'So you see, madame, it's as well to give in my resignation now, so that you can advertise for a replacement who can begin in the New Year.'

Madame Gebermann gave a groan. 'If you knew how many times I have been through that process, Clarissa! I dread to think what Monsieur Pagel will say!'

'I'm sorry, Madame Gebermann. I understand your difficulties. But my mind is made up.'

'Very well.'

166

When Clarissa got back to the office she shared with Babette she found her colleague waiting for her like a hunter watching a cave-opening. 'Clarissa! Where have you been? What did you mean by stalking out like that?'

'I've handed in my notice.'

'*Hi-hou!* You've done what?'

'Handed in my notice.'

'Clarissa—without telling me?' Babette's blue eyes filled with tears. 'I thought we were friends!'

'Oh, don't!' Clarissa put an arm round her shoulders. 'Don't take it like that, *chérie*. It isn't something I could discuss. I just suddenly felt—'

'But why, Clarissa? I thought you were enjoying life with us here at Entreprise Pagel—'

'Yes, yes, I was—I love working with you, and all the friends I've made in Geneva are important to me. But all at once I knew I couldn't stay any longer—'

'Clarissa!' Babette's voice, trembling with tears, almost broke. 'You're not saying that you're leaving Geneva?'

'I think it would be best, Babette—'

'No, no—how can you say that? Best for whom? I shall miss you terribly, and poor Edouard—'

'Edouard is going to have to learn to live without me some time, Babette—it might as well be sooner than later.'

'That's all wrong and you know it! Edouard relies on you to give him a sense of individuality—'

'He'll still have you, Babette.'

'But—but—'

The telephone shrilled over her incoherent protest. Clarissa picked it up.

'Mademoiselle Oakley?' said Madame Gebermann's voice. 'Monsieur Pagel would like to speak to you at once.'

Clarissa had to swallow hard before she replied. 'Yes, *madame*, I'll come immediately.'

As she replaced the receiver Babette said, '*Le patron?*'

'Yes.'

'Withdraw your resignation, Clarissa! Tell him it

was a mistake.'

Clarissa couldn't help smiling. 'A mistake? No one types out a resignation by mistake.'

'Then say you just weren't feeling well—a *crise de nerfs*, a sudden mood. He'll understand.'

'Do you think he would? It's not the kind of behaviour he's sympathetic to.'

'But he'd overlook it—he won't want you to go.'

Clarissa had a sudden glorious vision of Roland saying: 'Please don't leave. I can't manage without you.' But it went almost as soon as it came. Roland Pagel was never going to use words like that to Clarissa Oakley.

Madame Gebermann ushered her straight through the outer office and into Roland's. He was sitting at his desk with the sheet of paper on which she had typed her resignation on the blotter in front of him. As Madame Gebermann left them he picked up the paper.

'What is the meaning of this?' he inquired.

'I wish to leave my employment here.'

'For what reason?'

'I don't have to give a reason, sir. I just wish to go.'

'Is it more money? Is it simply that you feel you are worth more? If so, you are a little impatient. Our policy is to review the salaries of new employees at the end of six months—your review is due at the end of January.'

'That's not—'

'However, since it isn't important, I am prepared to increase your salary as from—'

'It isn't more money, Monsieur Pagel,' said Clarissa, more hurt than she could say by such an imputation. 'I simply wish to leave for personal reasons.'

He stared at her. His face was grim and, she thought, rather pale. 'Madame Gebermann voiced one or two ideas to me. She said that . . . you may be leaving Switzerland.'

'Yes.'

She was determined not to say more. Her manner was brittle and abrupt.

'When are you going?'

'My present plan is to go home for Christmas and stay

awhile.'

'And after that?'

'The future is still not quite mapped out.'

'I see.' He rose from his desk, went to the window, and gazed out. She knew that far below him he could see the lake, a sheet of pewter-grey under cloudy skies. The leaves had almost gone from the trees on its shore walks. Gone was the profusion of blossoms whose colour had made a border of grace and charm round the ever-changing waters. Winter was coming.

After a moment, without turning back, Roland spoke.

'I think you are making a great mistake, Miss Oakley, but of course it is not my business to give you advice. If you wish to leave I cannot prevent you. But it *is* my business to prevent disruption of my office routine. You have certain projects under your control, notably the English translation of the handbook—'

'Yes, sir—it's at the printers now.'

'I am aware of that. The proofs are expected in about ten days. I wish you to read them and make any necessary corrections, and to see the handbook through to a finished product.'

'But I—'

'You have to give a month's notice, Miss Oakley. That should give you time.'

'I would rather leave at once, if it is convenient.'

'It is *not* convenient. You will stay and fulfil your contract.'

'Very well, Monsieur Pagel.'

'That is all, Miss Oakley.'

He didn't turn round as she walked out.

CHAPTER X

Clarissa had only been home about an hour that evening when her doorbell rang. Outside were Babette and Edouard.

'I phoned him,' Babette explained. 'We've come to

talk some sense into you.'

'Oh, please, Babette—'

'I d-don't understand why you behaved so impulsively,' said Edouard. 'It's not like you.'

'And what about your career? Didn't you tell me you wanted to use your job at Entreprise Pagel as a springboard to greater things?'

'How do you know I haven't got a better job lined up?' Clarissa countered.

'Have you?'

'Not yet,' she said, unwilling to tell white lies.

Edouard took her hand with surprising firmness and sat down with her on the sofa.

'Clarissa, will you tell me something frankly?'

'If I can, Edouard.' She looked into his earnest eyes.

'Simone says you're going to marry Jean-Louis Blech. Is that why you're leaving your job?'

'Oh, good heavens no!' she burst out. She couldn't bear to let him think that—she knew it would grieve him deeply. 'It's to get away from things like that that I'm leaving Geneva!'

'What do you mean?' gasped Babette.

'I'm just so sick and tired—! It's almost as if I can't call my soul my own! Everyone seems to want to throw me into Jean-Louis' arms, and that's one of the things I can't bear—'

'You don't love Jean-Louis?'

'Of course not!'

'But Simone says—'

'Simone, Simone! Will you explain to me why you pay so much heed to your sister, Edouard? She's just a woman like any other. She can be wrong—'

'But Papa says she's exceptional—'

'That may be true, but you're exceptional too, Edouard—and much nicer!'

'What?'

'Nicer,' agreed Babette. 'Hadn't that ever occurred to you?'

'But, Babette—'

'Listen, we came here to browbeat Clarissa. If Jean-Louis is a problem to her—'

'He certainly is,' said, Clarissa, quite happy to accentuate that side of the affair so that no one should suspect her real reason. 'At the party on Saturday night he was carrying on as if we'd named the day, and he just doesn't seem to believe me when I tell him it isn't going to happen.'

'But if you tell him straight—?'

'Have *you* tried talking to Jean-Louis, Babette? I just don't seem to get through to him. If I could tell him that I don't even like him it would be easier, but oddly enough I'm quite fond of him, despite all the problems he's brought with him.'

'You'll just have to be ruthless.'

'I *am* being ruthless. I'm going away.'

For almost an hour they argued back and forth, but Clarissa was adamant. She would not withdraw her resignation. She was determined to leave in a month's time.

As Babette and Edouard said good night she could see they were headed for a long talk-session together. There was some comfort in that, at least. Her departure would bring them closer together.

After a poor night's sleep she rose thankfully at a rather early hour and wrote home to her mother, telling her the news. Daylight was coming as she posted the letter in the Place Longemalle. She walked down to the Pont Mont Blanc; the sun came up over the peaks, flooding the lake with light and tinting to pale rose the snow on the summits.

The snow-cap was moving down the mountains. The air this morning had a decided nip in it. After the gales and rain, a calm cold atmosphere held the valley in its tranquil grip. Clarissa went for a brisk walk along the Promenade du Lac, conscious for the first time that she would soon be leaving all this and knowing a deep regret at the thought.

She was in good time at the office, but Babette, surprisingly, was late. She came in looking flushed and worried.

'Clarissa, I'm afraid there's going to be trouble!'

'How do you mean?'

'Edouard rang me this morning. He was all keyed up. He said he'd decided to see Jean-Louis and knock some sense into him.'

Slowly Clarissa got up from her desk. 'I don't exactly follow—?'

'Last night he and I went to a café and talked and talked. It was after midnight when we said good night. Edouard kept saying that it was all wrong you should be forced out of Geneva—out of your job and the place you've made for yourself among us—by Jean-Louis' selfishness. He seems to have spent the night brooding about it.'

'Yes, but—'

'This morning he phoned. He hardly gave me time to say a word—really, Clarissa, it was quite unlike him! He said he was going up into the mountains to see Jean-Louis and knock some sense into him.'

Clarissa ran a hand through her hair. 'But didn't you try to stop him?'

'Of course! I tried to argue, but he wouldn't listen. Then I said I'd go too—I thought if I was there I could help to cool the situation. But he just replied that the track was pretty bad and it would be rough going in his little car, so he'd rather go alone. And hung up!'

'Where? Do you know where he was going?'

Babette shook her head miserably.

'How did Edouard know where to find Jean-Louis?'

'I've no idea.' The other girl had reached such a pitch of distress that she seemed scarcely capable of thinking.

'It must have been an assignment for Simone,' said Clarissa, more to herself than Babette. 'Jean-Louis must be out doing some photographic job and Simone must have mentioned the place.' She grabbed the phone and dialled Simone at the Chaval offices.

'Simone,' she said when she had been put through, 'where is Jean-Louis today?'

'Who's speaking? Oh, it's you, Clarissa!' Simone's voice, crisp and assured, took on a tinge of amusement. 'Keeping tabs on him, are you?'

'Simone, this is urgent. I'm trying to prevent a very

unpleasant scene. *Where* is Jean-Louis?'

For once Simone's confidence was shaken. 'At our newest site—La Berlue—Sparkling Rock Hotel. Why?'

'Thank you!' said Clarissa, and clashed the receiver down. She turned to Babette. 'It's all right—I know how to prevent the clash. I'll reach there ahead of Edouard and get Jean-Louis to take me somewhere—to Glion for lunch or something. By that time Edouard will have cooled down.'

Without pausing for discussion she seized her handbag from her desk, caught up her coat from the rack as she went past, and was going down in the lift a moment later. When the doors opened at the ground floor she found Roland Pagel waiting to step in. With a muttered good morning she hurried past him, aware that he turned to stare after her as she went out of the building at a time when she should have been starting her day's work.

At the corner she was lucky enough to catch a taxi at once, and was whisked to Cornavin Station in time for the eight forty-five train, which she caught with about two seconds to spare. An hour or so later she stepped out at Montreux and crossed the station to the MGL platform. It seemed a long twenty minutes before the little blue train trundled out on its trip up the mountain, but she knew she was still ahead of Edouard.

According to Babette, Edouard was going up to La Berlue by car. The drive to Montreux would take him about two hours, then he would have to head into the high gradients. Even if the road had been good it would probably have taken him another hour to get up to La Berlue by the zigzag mountain route.

Clarissa's plan was to go across the ravine by the cablecar which, if she remembered rightly, ran every hour on the half-hour. She should reach La Berlue by about ten minutes to eleven, when Edouard would still be coming up from Montreux.

She scuttled out of the MGL train at Toveyre hoping for transport of some sort to take her round to Jussaux, but no one was about—only two passengers boarding the train to go on up to Glion or Caux. There was nothing to do but walk; it wasn't far, after all.

She arrived at Jussaux breathless and alarmed. Her watch showed ten-thirty exactly, and knowing the Swiss devotion to punctuality she expected to see the cablecar sailing off without her. But as she took the half dozen concrete steps up to the ramp and the ticket office, she saw the car still in its bay, with the car-man putting packages aboard.

She bought her ticket. The man at the *guichet* said: 'You're lucky. There's a five-minute delay.'

'Thank goodness,' she gasped. 'Am I the only passenger?'

'It seems so.'

She watched while the last parcel was stowed.

'*V'la, mademoiselle*,' said the car-man, handing her aboard. Clarissa went in and sat on the hard wooden seat that ran round the interior. The driver took up his stance at the control panel. A pause ensued.

'Anything wrong?' she inquired.

'Oh no. They've been carrying out a correction on the cable tension this morning, that's all. I'm just waiting for the signal.'

A glance at her watch showed that the delay had now lasted seven minutes, which was a little unusual. Clarissa knew that all these little railways and cable-cars in the mountain ran, as a rule, precisely to the minute. A few weeks ago she had arrived two minutes too late for the Mont Pélerin funicular, and had stood by in annoyance as the last car went down the rails at twenty past eleven on the dot, leaving her to walk round to the main road in the dark and by good luck catch the last autobus.

Of course, in bad weather, all services in the Alps were subject to delay or cancellation. But today was calm and clear; the rain and wind of the stormy period were gone.

But just as she was about to query the position, the reciprocal bell rang from La Berlue, the driver turned his switch, and the car slid out on its line of cable. The terminus receded, to look like a little concrete box patched on to the mountain slope. Below them, the rocks of the ravine became visible; the grey-brown waters of a stream foaming over boulders looked like a crumpled satin ribbon. The tops of trees, scantily clad with leaves except for the conifers, looked like an uneven cushion.

'No snow up here yet?' Clarissa inquired, to make conversation.

'A thin cover behind La Berlue,' the car-man said. 'It's been mostly rain so far. A very wet November up here, *mademoiselle*.'

'It's been rather wet down on Lac Leman.'

'So I hear. But it's worse up here, you know. The rain runs down the slopes in torrents. I like it better around January—snow is easier to live with!'

Clarissa smiled, then turned again to look at La Berlue, which was above them on the higher side of the gorge. Slowly it was growing nearer—a little concrete box exactly like Jussaux, but at a greater altitude on a more perpendicular cliff.

The cable-car gave a lurch and then made a juddering move forward. At once an alarm bell rang out. A red light flashed on the driver's control panel. He slammed his switch to the 'off' position. The bell stopped, the red light stopped. With a quick sidelong glance at Clarissa he unhooked a handset from his panel of instruments.

'*Allo!* La Berlue, *qu'est-ce que se pase? Comment?*'

Clarissa had jumped to her feet as the car came to a standstill. She threw out a hand in alarm, and the driver, still listening to his phone, caught it in his. He gave it a reassuring squeeze. After a moment he began to speak into the handset, glancing out of the window as he did so. He spoke in the mountain dialect that she couldn't understand, but by following his gaze she guessed what he was saying.

The cable was strung between huge stanchions on either side of the gorge. These stanchions in their turn were kept at the correct angle by hawsers of steel rope like the guy-ropes that keep a tent upright. One of these hawsers had torn its concrete fixing-block from the shelf of rock in which it was embedded, so the cable had sagged out of alignment.

'*Oui, oui, j'comprends. Va bien. J'attends.*'

'Wait? For what?' Clarissa asked in a trembling

175

voice.

'They have to go down and look at the support,' he explained, pointing. 'They can estimate the strain when they get down there. The rain, you see—it's got into a fissure under the block of concrete and weakened the grip of the whole thing so that it's pulled loose.'

'How—how long will it take them to put it right?'

'Oh, an hour, I suppose. Maybe an hour and a half.'

'An hour and a half?' Clarissa echoed in horror. 'Have we just got to hang here in space for an hour and a half?'

'Now be sensible,' said the driver with severity. 'What else can we do?'

Nothing else, naturally. Clarissa sat down on the wooden bench and tried not to see the vast expanse of valley outside the glass of the little metal box in which they were suspended. Sunshine gleamed on the beige and grey rocks. Between the peaks, the sky was duck-egg blue flecked with feathery white clouds. A beautiful day, a mountaineer's day.

'Mind if I smoke?' inquired the car-man.

'Please do.'

He produced a pipe, filled it, had trouble getting it alight, then began to puff with satisfaction. 'There's nothing to worry about,' he assured her. 'One guy-rope has lost its tension, but there are five others on that side and six on the side we've just left. We're as safe as houses.'

'It's all right for you,' Clarissa said ruefully. 'I suppose you're used to this kind of thing!'

He was shocked. 'Nothing of the sort, I assure you! This is only the second time in my life I've been stuck, and I've been in this work over twenty years. I've been snowed in up on Pilatus, I admit, and once when I was on leave I got called out to replace a sick driver and found a bridge closed near Diablerets, but this makes the second hold-up on the cable that I've experienced, that's all.'

'What exactly will they do?'

'Well, they'll examine the displaced "grip" and see if they can put a temporary brace on it.'

'How's that done?'

176

'They bring a motor winch in, and wind the cable . . .'

'Bring in equipment? How long will that take?'

'Ah . . . Um . . . Depends how far it has to come. But then,' he added quickly, 'they may decide the stanchion is safe enough with only the five support ropes, in which case they'll bring us in. And that could be just a matter of an hour or two.'

Clarissa noticed that his estimate of time was casually being enlarged as he discussed the matter, but she made no comment. She was intelligent enough to understand that a cable-car couldn't be whisked in to its terminus like a trolleybus. She also understood that her friend the driver was not going to tell her anything that would alarm her.

'What's your name?' she inquired.

'Pierre Falaise.'

'I'm Clarissa Oakley.'

They bowed to each other.

'*Eh, bien,* Mademoiselle Oakley, would you care for a cup of coffee?' he inquired, and began to unscrew the top of a vacuum flask.

An hour later it was distinctly colder inside the cable-car. A wind was sighing and keening through the crevices at the edge of the windows, the wind betokened by those feathery clouds in the clear sky above the peaks.

On the rock-shelf below La Berlue, two men were examining the uprooted concrete block. Another was coming down a rock staircase from the terminus. Pierre Falaise had had two conversations on his intercom, after each of which he had assured Clarissa that the car would soon be reeled in.

Time went by. The trio of engineers stood together, like miniature soldiers on a contour table in a war game. One of them walked away to the edge of the rock shelf, spoke into a walkie-talkie.

About a quarter of an hour later a steady throbbing began to grow in the air somewhere to the east. A speck appeared, to resolve itself into a helicopter. It droned overhead, stopped a moment, then moved up and along the face of the ravine. Quite clearly the occupant was surveying the other supports of the stanchion on the

Sparkling Rock side of the valley. For some minutes it bustled back and forth, like one of the enormous dragon-flies that Clarissa had admired by the lakeshore.

Then it rose out of the valley and disappeared over the lip of the La Berlue cliff.

'What happens now?' Clarissa asked.

'I don't know. I expect they'll tell me—' He was interrupted by a ring from his phone. A phlegmatic conversation ensued. '*Bien sûr*,' he said in agreement with something from the other end. '*Un moment*.' He looked at Clarissa. 'The news services are asking if there are any passengers and have been told there is one. They want to know your name. I'm ordered to ask if I can tell them.'

'Why not?' said Clarissa, then added at once: 'My friends will be alarmed, though.'

'That's inevitable, but the message to the news services is that we are quite safe.'

She nodded agreement. Pierre relayed her name and her Geneva address. When he had hung up he went on: 'It may be a while. It seems there's a bit of movement in the sub-stratum.'

'What does that mean?'

'A crack is forming under some of the other supports. It's all due to the bad weather this autumn. Water has seeped through in much larger quantities than usual, I think. Ah well, not to worry. We'll soon be home.'

The time was then two o'clock in the afternoon. About three-thirty it began to get dark. That was when Clarissa began to grow really frightened.

'Couldn't they get us out by helicopter?' she asked through stiff lips.

Pierre looked troubled. 'It wouldn't be safe to try, not in this wind. The valley is like a funnel, you see—the helicopter blades have only to touch the cable by being blown against it, and down it would go.'

'I see. So what will they do?'

'They'll pull us in with a winch.'

'Soon?'

Pierre cleared his throat. 'It's not very likely, *mademoiselle*. They won't be able to see what they're doing in the dark.'

'Can't they bring lights up?'

'They're doing that. The army is supplying search-lights. Don't worry, Mademoiselle Clarissa—everything possible is being done.'

It was no longer feasible to see the activity on the rock surface below La Berlue; everything had faded from sight in the Alpine dusk. Pierre switched on an overhead light in the cabin. It struck Clarissa that from the cable-car stations on either side the cabin must now be sparkling like a Christmas light on a string.

'There's an old music hall song in England that just suits us,' she remarked. ' "She's only a bird in a gilded cage. A beautiful sight to see . . ." ' She began to laugh weakly, but the laughter changed to a sob.

'Don't cry, Mademoiselle Clarissa,' said Pierre anxiously. 'Everything will be all right.'

'I'm not crying,' said Clarissa, scrubbing with a fierce hand at the tears on her cheek, 'it's just that I'm s-so c-cold!'

The phone on the control panel buzzed. Pierre answered it, then in amazement held it out.

'It's for you, *mademoiselle*,' he said.

'Me? What do you mean?'

'Someone asking to speak to Mademoiselle Oakley,' he insisted.

In utter amazement she took the handset and held it to her ear. 'Hullo?' she faltered.

'Clarissa? Thank God! Don't worry, Clarissa—we'll have you out of there in no time!'

Now it was no use trying to hold back the tears. At the sound of that blessed, blessed voice, all barriers went down.

'Oh, Roland, please hurry! It's so awful, Roland—it's so dark!' She hunched forward as sobs shook her. Pierre Falaise put his arms round her and held her steady. Supported by his arms and with the phone jammed against his uniformed chest, Clarissa listened as Roland Pagel promised on his own life and the life of his mother that he would have her safe on firm ground as soon as humanly possible.

'Don't be afraid,' he said. 'There's nothing to be afraid of. I promise, Clarissa—I promise.'

Because he promised, she choked back her tears. She knew he would never fail her.

CHAPTER XI

Nevertheless the grey dawn of the winter mountains was creeping into the sky before the cable-car began to move. Twelve hours had gone by—twelve terrible hours of cold and isolation. It had been impossible to sleep even though Clarissa and Pierre had huddled together among the packages on the floor. From time to time, staring out of the windows, they could see lights on the La Berlue side, and figures moving about. But then the windows frosted over; it was no longer possible to look out. Clarissa scarcely knew whether to be glad or sorry.

At four information came through on the phone: equipment from the Pagel construction site had been transferred along the cliff to the terminus, the Army had sent in lights and a portable dynamo. Drums of cable had been hoisted into place by helicopter. As soon as there was enough light to see what they were doing they would begin the recovery of the cable-car.

From then on there was no question of trying to sleep again. Pierre and Clarissa sat on the cartons inside the cabin, as far from the cold outer walls as possible. Clarissa was wearing a good thick coat of Yorkshire tweed, the car-man had a topcoat of loden cloth: even so they had trouble keeping their teeth from chattering.

Soon after six came further instructions by phone. At seven the car began to move. Clarissa was too scared to look—she sat with eyes shut tight and fists clenched as the car shuddered and swayed and then, almost imperceptibly, began to inch forward.

It seemed to take a century. She learned afterwards it had taken one hour and eighteen minutes to cover the half-space between Jussaux and La Berlue, the crossing of which in its entirety usually took seventeen minutes. As they dandled slowly into the docking bay, Clarissa could see a group on the concrete ramp—two news-cameramen, four or five men in the protective helmets of construction work, an army engineering officer and three soldiers, a girl bundled up in a borrowed donkey-jacket—and Roland. He stood head and shoulders above the others, shading his eyes to try for a glimpse of the car's occupants.

The cable-car drifted to a stop. The sliding door sighed open. Pierre Falaise stepped out, then turned to help Clarissa. Eager hands grasped her. The cold fresh air hit her cheeks. A blanket was draped around her. She heard Babette's voice: 'Clarissa! Oh, Clarissa dear!'

Her legs buckled under her. Her day had ended almost as soon as it had begun.

When she opened her eyes again she saw the ceiling of her own room in Geneva. She stirred. A figure moved —Madame Lallais.

'*Eh bien*, you've come back to us, eh? How do you feel?'

Clarissa closed her eyes and opened them again. 'Very odd,' she said. 'Have I been asleep?'

'More or less. The doctor gave you a sedative.'

She looked at the ceiling. Lamplight. 'What time is it?'

'Six-thirty.'

'What day?'

'Thursday.'

'Thursday?' She had been trapped in the cable-car on Tuesday morning, rescued at dawn on Wednesday. 'What happened to the time in between?' she asked.

'You've spent it in bed. And let me tell you you'll spend tomorrow there, too.'

'Have you been looking after me?'

'*Certainement*. Now, are you hungry?'

'I am, rather,' Clarissa confessed. 'What have you got to offer—that famous *longeole?*' She laughed, and was surprised to find that it came out in a curious creaking sound.

'We'll have some soup,' said Madame Lallais reprovingly, 'and perhaps a little omelette. Would you like that?'

'I'd love it.' But oddly enough, though she thought she was hungry, she had soon had enough. Eating was too tiring. She wanted to lie down again. She drank the hot milk and cognac that Madame Lallais brought, and drifted off to sleep again.

When she woke again it was daylight, early morning by the looks of it, and she felt much better. She sat up; this time her head didn't swim. She looked at the bedside clock—eight a.m. Normally she would be on her way to the office. Gingerly she got out of bed, pulled her dressing-gown about her, and went to the window.

The sun was beginning to cast shafts of light in the narrow lane. From the construction site farther up the hill came the sounds of activity. Outside the gate in the fence a car was parked—a dark blue Lamborghini. Roland was there, visiting the site, then. Clarissa was about to open the window and lean out, to see if she could see him, when a shriek of horror from Madame Lallais made her turn.

'What are you doing out of bed? Get back at once, *méchant enfant!* The doctor said you were not to get up until Saturday.'

The old lady shooed her into bed like a mother-hen looking after its chick.

'But you're feeling better, yes? You look better.'

'I feel fine.'

'Ah, what it is to be young! Eighteen hours hanging up in the cold, yet after a couple of days' rest you don't even have a sneeze. Well, can you eat breakfast?'

'I could eat *two* breakfasts.'

'Very well, I shall bring you two breakfasts, also many letters and cards and telephone messages, and the newspaper with your photo.'

Clarissa was deeply touched and a little astonished at the number of messages of concern that had come in. Even plump old Gottfried Zucher and his wife had sent a basket of Parma violets and a card. There were greetings from Madame Gebermann and others at the office, a fluffy troll-like creature from Babette, and a telegram from her parents to say: 'Thank God all well, please come home for rest, fondest love.'

Perhaps she wasn't as fully recovered as she thought. She felt strangely weepy as she opened first one envelope, then another. She might have been looking for one particular message, and when she found it she could scarcely see it for the tears that filled her eyes.

It was tucked in a box containing a sprig of white heather fixed to a little silver clip. The message on the card ran: 'This is for safe journeying—Roland Pagel.' Clarissa took it out of the box and held it against the shoulder of her nightdress. 'For safe journeying.' Yes, he had remembered that she was leaving.

During the day she had quite a stream of visitors. At lunchtime came Madame Gebermann with a huge basket of fruit and the message that she was not expected back at Entreprise Pagel. 'Monsieur Pagel will fall in with your wishes, whatever you decide to do, Mademoiselle Oakley. He feels . . . well, he feels that in the circumstances you must make your own decision.'

'I see. Thank you, Madame Gebermann.' Clarissa gathered her thoughts. The doctor had said she ought to have a week's rest, and her parents had begged her to come home. Since she had intended to be home for Christmas, perhaps it was better to go now. 'In that case, would you mind if we regard my resignation as taking effect immediately? I don't really feel up to coming back, and it hardly seems worth it anyhow.'

Madame Gebermann nodded agreement. She would send various documents via Babette, who was calling that evening.

Babette was divided between delight at seeing Clarissa alive and well, and tears at the notion that in two days' time she would be gone. 'If your mind is made up,' she sighed, 'I suppose it's no use arguing. But as a matter of fact, Clarissa, one of your problems is solved. Edouard put Jean-Louis straight about how you really felt, and Jean-Louis has agreed not to be a nuisance any more.'

'You mean Edouard actually confronted Jean-Louis?

After all my efforts to prevent a row?'

'There wasn't a row. Edouard arrived up at La
Berlue to find everybody—well, I mean, the few people
up there—staring at the cable-car and wondering what
to do. Jean-Louis was one of them. In the circumstances it hardly seemed right to begin a shouting-match.
Of course they'd no *idea* that *you* were in the cable-car.
That fact didn't emerge until the newsmen wanted the
passenger's name. Then it came over on the telephone,
and from all I hear both Edouard and Jean-Louis nearly
died of shock then and there.'

'How did you come on the scene?' Clarissa asked.

'Oh—good gracious—don't remind me. My mother
rang me at the office—she heard it on the radio about
three o'clock. I suppose I lost my head. I went rushing
in to Madame Gebermann and while I was trying to
explain to her, Monsieur Pagel came storming out,
demanding to know what all the noise was about. I
made a hash of trying to explain. He picked up a phone,
was put through to a friend in Radio Romande, got the
latest information, and was out of the door *so fast*—! I
went galloping after him, clutching at his coat. Imagine,
Clarissa! Clutching at Monsieur Pagel!'

'And he took you with him?'

'We flew in. We went up in a light plane from
Geneva Airport. I think it took ten minutes!' Babette
giggled. 'I didn't have time to get frightened before we
had landed on a slope on the north side of La Berlue and
were in a jeep grinding up the track to the cable-car
terminus. Then after that all I did was make coffee for
the men and scramble eggs and so on—there were food
supplies at the construction site for the new ski hotel. I
didn't really see much of what went on. It's just as
well really. Edouard and I kept busy, and then when
the cable-car was brought in Monsieur Pagel rounded
us up and told me to be ready in case you needed me.'

'I remember hearing your voice.'

'I made a fool of myself, crying all over you. It was
Monsieur Pagel who caught you when you collapsed. Ah
well, he's more accustomed to crises than I am.' Babette
shook her head over her recollections. 'I must say I'm

not so scared of him now. I can even see what it is that makes La Masagram want him so much.'

Babette collected signatures on various documents terminating Clarissa's appointment; these she had to deliver to Entreprise Pagel on Monday morning. She arranged to come back next day to help Clarissa pack, and when that was accomplished insisted on seeing her off at the airport on Sunday. Others came with her: Edouard, rather quiet but full of good wishes for her future, and old Madame Lallais who was almost as excited at visiting the airport as she was distressed by Clarissa's departure.

It was strange how soon she was home. At London Airport she changed planes for Newcastle; her parents met her there.

'Goodness, how pale you are! Are you sure you were well enough to travel?'

'Quite sure, Mother. I'm a bit tired now, that's all.'

On the drive out to the little moorland town Clarissa was silent. Outside the car a dark landscape slipped by —not the mountains and the lakeshore of Geneva but the old familiar countryside of rolling fields and bracken-covered slopes. Now that December had come, perhaps there would be snow. A white Christmas ... Not so white as Christmas in the Alps, of course. But it was no use thinking about that—it was all in the past now.

There was no snow. The weather was unseasonably mild. Clarissa went out walking, exercised the Labrador dog, went to bed early and slept badly. By Wednesday she was so well settled in her old surroundings that she began on a task she had been putting off—thank-you letters to all the friends in Switzerland.

First she wrote to the cable-car driver, Pierre Falaise, to express her gratitude for his kindness and stolid courage during their ordeal. Then she wrote to everyone who had sent a message while she was recovering. She even wrote to Roland: 'It was kind of you to send the white heather, but more deeply still I appreciate the way you came to help at La Berlue. I hope you will find a new secretary for the English correspondence without too much trouble.' She had headed it: 'Monsieur Pagel' and wasn't sure whether to sign it 'Clarissa' or 'Clarissa Oakley'. In the end she left it open, feeling that she could decide later.

Last she had to write to Jean-Louis, in reply to a letter from him that had arrived at her Geneva address before she left.

'Now that I understand how much I embarrassed you, I can only marvel at your forbearance. The last thing I wanted was to drive you away, Clarissa, but perhaps we would have said goodbye in any case. I have decided to make the break, to go away before our hideous Swiss winter takes hold of me. I see now that you never would have come with me to Florida, but that won't prevent me from being lonely for you there. Yet I know—as I suppose you do—that I'll get over it. At the moment— yes—I'm unhappy. But I'll be less unhappy if you can write me a line saying you forgive me.'

There was a great deal of pathos in that, but how much was genuine and how much was calculated Clarissa couldn't tell. She doubted whether Jean-Louis himself knew. The best thing was to reply in rather a brisk vein, wishing him well, and this she did.

She sealed and stamped all the letters except the one to Roland. Somehow she couldn't bring herself to seal it; it was a final goodbye once she had done so, and to keep even such a tenuous link as 'owing him a letter' was better than nothing.

She gathered up the rest and called Dreamer the Labrador—so called because he spent most of his time asleep—for a walk to the postbox. She was just fetching his lead when her attention was caught by the sound of a car in the lane. It was quite normal for a car to draw up outside, but there was something about the sound of this one that struck her as unusual. She went to the window of the sitting-room.

A dark blue Lamborghini!

She felt herself go cold, then hot, then cold again. Transfixed, she watched as an unmistakable figure un- coiled himself from the driving-seat. He opened the garden gate, walked up the path.

Dreamer, hearing strange footsteps, lolloped eagerly to

the door and stood with his nose against the handle. Clarissa's mother called from the kitchen, 'Someone at the door, dear. I hear Dreamer there.'

'Yes, Mother.' Shivering as if in a fever, Clarissa went into the passage. Her hands trembled so much she could scarcely lift the latch.

'Good afternoon,' said Roland. 'How are you, Clarissa?'

'Oh—quite well, thank you.' She stood aside. 'Won't you come in?'

'Thank you.' He stepped past her. Dreamer bumped enthusiastically against him. 'Good gracious, what an enormous animal!'

'His name is Dreamer.'

'Who is it, dear?' called her mother.

'It's Monsieur Pagel, Mother.'

'Who?'

'Monsieur Pagel. From Geneva.'

There was an unbelieving pause. Then Mrs Oakley came into the passage with a bowl of bulbs in her hand.

'Monsieur Pagel?' she gasped. 'From Geneva?'

'How do you do, Mrs Oakley?'

'I won't shake hands,' said Mrs Oakley. 'I'm planting my Christmas bulbs.'

'Really? Isn't it rather late?'

'Better late than never, I always say.' She looked in bewilderment at this unexpected visitor.

'I brought Clarissa some work she omitted to finish,' he explained. Under his arm he was carrying a thick buff envelope, which he now offered to Clarissa. 'The proofs of the English translation.'

'Oh, I see.' Quite satisfied, Clarissa's mother turned away. 'I expect you've got things to talk about. If you'll excuse me, I'll get on with my bulbs.'

'By all means,' said Roland with a sudden smile.

Clarissa ushered him into the sitting-room. Dreamer, having seen them safely installed, lay down in the doorway and prepared for a nap.

'You didn't come all the way from Geneva just to deliver proofs,' she said in a husky voice.

'Of course not. I came to see you. I wanted to be

sure you were all right.'

'I'm quite recovered, thank you.'

'You've been writing letters, I see. Did you write to me?'

'Yes,' she said, shuffling all the envelopes into a heap.

'What did you say, Clarissa?' He put his hands on her shoulders and looked down at her with a glance that scared her. 'What did you say? It couldn't be that you are getting married soon to Jean-Louis, because Babette told me you were leaving Switzerland to *get away* from Jean-Louis.'

Clarissa gazed up at him in confusion. 'But I never suggested I was marrying Jean-Louis.'

'You said you were leaving my employment because you were going to Florida with Jean-Louis.'

'I didn't! Roland, I didn't say that!'

His fingers dug into her shoulders almost cruelly. 'Didn't you tell Madame Gebermann that when you were married you wouldn't have to fit your work as a housewife round your job at Entreprise Pagel, because you were going to Florida?'

'No! No, truly—how could she have thought I said that? I never mentioned Florida to Madame Gebermann. I told her I was leaving Switzerland. But I meant—leaving for home.'

Suddenly he let her go and sank into a chair. 'Clarissa,' he said, 'in the name of everything you hold dear, explain to me! I can't go on like this!' He ran a hand across his eyes. 'It's like living in a nightmare—one of those terrible dreams when you try and try to catch up with someone, but never succeed.'

'Roland—' Overcome by concern, she knelt beside him. 'I don't know what there is to explain. Please listen to me'—she caught his sleeve in her two hands—'I have never—*never*—felt anything except a gentle affection for Jean-Louis Blech. In the last few weeks he suddenly took it into his head that he was in love with me. That was after—' She broke off, colouring deeply. 'Well, I don't want to talk about that. The point is, he began talking as if he and I were to be married when he'd put together enough money to make a new start in a

188

sunny never-never-land. But I never wanted him to talk like that and I never wanted to marry him.'

'But Simone said . . .'

'Yes,' Clarissa murmured, 'Simone said . . . That was where you heard this talk about marrying and going to Florida.'

'But nevertheless . . . Clarissa . . . there is still a mystery. Why did you suddenly resign? Surely Madame Gebermann can't have been entirely mistaken in the reasons you gave? She spoke of a big change in your life.'

'Not *my* life, Roland.'

He took her face in his hands and turned it up so that he could look full into her eyes. 'Whose, then?'

'Yours, Roland.'

He gave a little shake of the head. 'Mine? I had only one change in mind—and that I had kept a secret, locked inside myself. What do you mean, *mon amour?* What change?'

Every fibre of her being thrilled at the words. '*Mon amour*'—my love. Like the beginning of a miracle, Clarissa felt the world changing before her eyes.

'Roland, I believed you were going to marry Simone Masagram.'

There was a long, long pause. Then he swept her up into his arms. 'Oh, you fool!' he whispered against her hair. 'You dear, benighted fool! It's you I love! It's you I want! Clarissa, you're my life!'

Some moments later the Labrador dog, sensing a difference in the atmosphere, arose in his lumbering fashion and came into the room waving his tail.

'Dreamer, you can be the first to congratulate us,' Roland told him, releasing Clarissa sufficiently to look down at him.

The dog, satisfied at being spoken to, wandered out. Clarissa said, 'He's probably as bewildered as I am. I can't *believe* it!'

'I find it difficult myself. In fact, it was inconceivable to me, but Madame Lallais insisted she knew best—so I came to find out.'

'Madame Lallais? How does she come into it?'

'I went to see her after you had gone. I had called once or twice while you were recovering from the accident—'

'I saw your car!' Clarissa interrupted. 'On Friday morning!'

'Yes. I came to the apartment that morning. Madame Lallais is a boisterous old lady—she says what she thinks, I can tell you. I called on Sunday to ask if all had gone well at the airport and she said you were gone, as much in love with me as ever.'

'Roland!' Clarissa buried her face against his jacket.

'So it makes you blush? Think what it did to me, *ma bien-aimée!* I suppose I looked shattered because she then went on to tell me that you had come back from your "excursion to the Château de Chillon" with your heart broken because someone had been unkind to you. "And if it wasn't you, Monsieur Pagel," she said, rapping me on the shoulder with her knuckles, "it certainly wasn't that worthless Monsieur Blech."'

'And you already knew it wasn't Jean-Louis . . .'

'Exactly, because Babette had explained how you felt, and that Édouard had been on the track of Jean-Louis, and that you were in that confounded cable-car expressly to prevent them having a fist-fight about it.' Roland groaned. 'That cable-car! It will haunt me all my life! If you knew how I felt when I got there . . .'

'Ssh,' said Clarissa, laying a finger on his lips, 'don't think about it. We'll only think about good things from now on.'

'Heaven knows we've enough bad things behind us,' he said with a sigh. 'When I think how angry I got with you, how I tried at first not to fall in love with you! Why, I even ran away to Milan at the outset to try to bring myself to reason!'

'Did you, my darling? Never mind, I was just as foolish. I kept on telling myself and telling myself that I mustn't fall in love with you, because I . . . well, to some extent I thought you were unlikely to marry anyone except Simone.'

'Ah yes . . . Simone. In a way that is like Jean-Louis. Simone has made herself believe that we are destined to be man and wife. But it could never happen, Clarissa. Even if I had never met you I could never have married Simone. Perhaps Fate always intended me for a calm, reticent English girl with amber eyes and hair the colour of ferns in autumn.'

'Fate sent me to Geneva,' said Clarissa. 'I see that now.'

'And love will keep you there, for ever and ever. I will make you happy, my dearest one, just as you will make my world a paradise.'

As he held her close she rested her lips against his cheek in a final sealing of their promise. She would live with him in their home above the lake of silver, in whose magical waters her love story had been reflected.

Harlequin Presents..

EACH MONTH –
FOUR GREAT NOVELS

Here are the Latest Titles:

ALL BOOKS 75c

These titles are available at your local bookseller, or through the Harlequin Reader Service, M.P.O. Box 707, Niagara Falls, N.Y. 14302; Canadian address 649 Ontario St., Stratford, Ont.

W